TRICIA LIFTON: A NOVELLA

By Saul Wheelock

Copyright

I.

The two sweet old men lay dead across the circulation desk. One had his head in his arms, the other had fallen across one of Smiscka's books. His hair fanned over the cover's black-and-white portrait of the philosopher grinning miserably and naked from a claw-footed bathtub, one bear-like arm swung over the porcelain rim.

The temperature had plunged again. On the other side of the tempered-glass doors, a guard sprawled over a pool of frozen blood like he was resting on a red oblong mirror. Coffee had rolled out of his cup, the frosted brown frustum coming to a stop against the tip of his nose. A pen jutted from his neck.

The library was quiet now. I could hear someone trembling, probably Teri. She said she would meet me in the children's section. I hadn't even known they had books for children.

I wandered between the shelves until I found a woman crouched with her head in her hands. Her fingers were working through her short-cropped white hair.

"Teri?"

Her eyes shot up, blinking with fear and confusion, then softened with affection. "Is it you?" she said. I recognized the voice. "My little artist?"

She pushed herself to her feet and approached me timidly.

"I always thought you were tiny," she said.

She reached for my cheek, then snapped together and became jittery in a different way. "Do you want to see what you've done?"

I shook my head, no. But she gestured behind her in a panic. "Your art?"

I had never seen my art before. My sketches, or whatever they were, were nothing more than black ink, fine lines with an ultrafine nib, finished with a few broad splashes of watercolor. I never thought of them as art.

Teri commissioned them. She'd call me on the mansion's

landline and ask me to do dogs or something. As soon as I hung up, I went to my studio in the attic and sat at a long wooden table surrounded by shelves of empty jars and reams of paper. I always looked forward to the moment before I started because I wasn't thinking about the past or the future. I chewed on my nails or played with my hair, my mind a blank. Eventually I made a few sketches with a light-lead pencil.

Circles became dog bowls or tires in a thatch of weeds, a crooked scratch would thicken into a tree trunk with cross-hatched bark or a hind leg cocked just so. I ran my thumb over the lines, smudging them for shadows and depth. Gray lines and gray smudges on crisp gray paper. Doodles, outlines, a way of rooting through the corners of my mind where messes collected. I raked aside the dried leaves, the smashed plastic bottles and torn newspaper to find whatever surprise was buried there, a doll with wide-staring eyes or a swollen notebook that had miraculously survived the damp, etched with pools of light blue.

Nobody came up to the attic. I was left to myself almost every day for—how long? Six years. A call from Teri, sketches and then ink and watercolors.

There was nothing more to it, other than the way the sun came through the windows. The sunlight changed over the course of the day. When I was tired and nearly done at dusk, the beams fell across the desk, a skein of velvety orange. The paper on the table glowed. Even when it was freezing outside, the room felt warm. In the middle of the day, as I scraped through the work, the light was less generous, squaring the studio with cloud-filtered light. The best light was in the morning. It was alive, speckled with motes like so many tiny ghosts caught on a shimmering highway between heaven and earth. I drank mugs of nettle tea, wondering what the pretty little ghosts were thinking, until the clouds barged up against one another.

Teri was watching me. "Are you ready?" she asked.

No. I wasn't. She beckoned me closer but I was lost in memories. Of when I was done. I'd cap the pen and stroke it across the page like I was filling in blank spots, sketching in details with the bald point, coloring it and completing it. But the opposite was happening. Whatever was mine was drawn out. The dog, or whatever it was, would become bare like someone shaved off its fur, stripping it of whatever depth it had. The picture would be thin and inert. It was like looking a picture of myself after I was dead—me but not me, mine but not mine—and wondering if anything had ever been there in the first place. The effect was irritating, like the paper was an extension of my skin, peeled off, itching but unscratchable.

That was the cue. I reached for the brush, dry as a twig, dabbed dusty cakes of pigment with distilled water, and gave each color a few pale inches of the page.

And that was it. A splash of color in place of an emotion, an emotion in place of nothing.

If the picture settled in my mind, it was done. I'd slip the paper between the flaps of a dismantled cardboard box and place it flat under a pile of bricks, a red and yellow cairn to mark the spot. It prevented the curls of wet color from puckering the paper. By morning, the pictures would be ready for a manila envelope printed with her address, and I'd send them and wait for Teri's next call.

I never asked what they were for. I was just grateful for something to do. One time she broke the rules and gave me her number. I memorized it but knew not to use it.

Teri was waving at a shelf behind her and saying something. The memories were pinched from me and vanished. All I could think about was how confusing everything was now that it all made sense. The emptiness, the murders, Ishi's private death, their patience and their impatience. It all made sense. Even Teri's compassion. Especially her compassion.

A cloud passed over the skylight and the library filled with dead light.

Something caught my eye, familiar but estranged, behind her. The books were bigger than the others in the library but thinner. Covers were blunted at the corner from being repeatedly dropped. Some had been repaired with yellowed strips of tape.

I saw a picture I had painted. And another, and another.

Teri looked from them to me, buzzing, "There. There. And there."

They didn't look exactly like mine. They were flatter and duller. I reached past her and picked one. Orchards, apples, a snake. I recognized the lines and the colors. The pages were thin, almost like tracing paper, but shiny white, and words were printed underneath, somebody else's words, a stranger's. I dropped the book and took another, flicked through it and dropped it.

They were all there. Lined up in shelves. I began pulling books out whether or not they had my pictures, opening them in a panic, as if something small and alive was trapped inside one of them and I was searching to free it. I let them fall from my hands when nothing came out.

But as I moved, the images stayed. I had never dreamed of the company my illustrations would keep. Some were beautiful. Children in pairs, willowy nuns, a dancing toad in a uniform, teddy bears, a pointy-nosed rat. Some were ugly. Stiff black figures on monochrome scarlet and black. Blocky cartoon elephants. I threw books down and grabbed more.

And amongst them, in this world, were my own, so familiar because I remembered drawing them and so estranged because they belonged to the words leading them away; they walked away, hand in hand with a new lover, casting incurious glances back.

I remembered each one. A bull under the belly of a rock outcropping. An old man holding a child by the hand. A rainstorm over a city square.

With memories came feelings. A sequence of squirrels in the crook of a tree made me tingle with the abstract happiness I felt when I painted it. I was just happy to be. With another—cats, slinky and chagrined—came contentment, so mildly pleasant it barely touched me. Others made me sob inside, a remote sadness that suddenly comes near. People who were gone came alive.

And then, with books piled around my feet, tented, broken-spined, the pictures stopped saying anything at all.

Teri had big tears in her eyes. "You needed to see this," she said. She was swelling with pride, affection, dread. And then in a scratchy voice, she said, "Can you see what I did for you?"

I held a book. One of my last. What would it have been like to read it as a child? To have been surrounded by these books? To have lived in a world of bright fruits and lopsided cities, zooming cars with puffs of exhaust and precipitously leaning buses, a world of zoos and parades, chatty animals, a world with no shadows, with bright yellow suns and pencil-thin trees, a world that seemed to be sorry and yet was without remorse, a world where the most frightening things were also pretty? What had children seen in these pictures?

Did they think I did this for them?

On the last page, underneath a bear cub with honeycomb, were two letters, CM.

Teri followed my gaze to the letters below the cub's paw.

"I never said anything," she whispered, "when you started signing them."

Did she think she was doing me a favor?

"I was glad you felt they belonged to you," she said.

But the initials belonged to another person. Not me. The clouds gave way and the room glowed as if the lights had been turned back on. CM was older than me, much older than I would ever be. CM didn't live in dormitories or hostels, CM had a cottage with a garden and was sent tea-colored letters, handwritten in ink that browned with age, stuffed into crisp envelopes, and stashed in the back of a cupboard. CM had a past and a future. Death was a mystery for Caye Mallory; Caye Mallory wouldn't even believe in death if it hadn't been for the letters.

That was the Caye Mallory who did these drawings. And that would never be me. I had just learned that it was all over.

It never occurred to me that I had been illustrating books, let alone books for children. What would it have been like to have been a child?

"You have a gift," said Teri. "It's why you were put here."

I slapped the book shut and pushed it into her hands. Teri stumbled back, unable to hide her terror any more than she could hide her good intentions. She knew what I was, she knew what I had become, and still she hoped to save me. But there was nothing left to save. There never had been.

I knelt at the foot of the shelf, now empty, a lattice of thin white metal strips, a suitable altar to say a very first prayer. On my knees on the broken carpet of books, my hair fell across my eyes and I clutched my hands to my chest.

"Please," I prayed to the bare metal, "let it all end soon."

II.

One Year Earlier

We'd left the car at a deserted parking lot and set off in the late afternoon. Our hats and clothing stuck to us in the heat. When the sun began sinking on the horizon, Ishi threw down her backpack.

"Why here?" I asked, looking over the red arenite plateau onto miles of fractured sand and shrubs. I was reluctant to stop. I wanted to move past the curious cramps and spasms in my calves and shoulders.

Ishi scanned the area and nodded with finality. The storm was gathering. She rubbed her forehead against her sleeve, leaving a grassy stain across the fabric. She smelled faintly of hay.

We erected the tent and regarded each other suspiciously as if we had hidden a secret expertise from one another.

But she was right. It was the perfect place. If she had not stopped us, I would have led us to our death, falling for the desert's trick of promising relief a few steps on, a few steps on, a few steps on.

We unpacked inside the tent. Whatever was with us was all we had left. Clothes mostly, wadded up. We glanced curiously and jealously at what the other managed to keep. Ishi showed me a tired teddy bear. It made sense. She was the last. She never acted like it but then she'd show up with her teddy bear. I showed her some paintbrushes. I didn't show her the letter I'd tucked into a slice in the fabric of my backpack.

When we were done sharing and hiding our secrets in the tent, we slipped out and started a fire. We drank water and ate and stared at the cobra of smoke suspended in a curvaceous dance over the yellow flame.

When we were done, Ishi put her hands on her tiny hips and stared out across the desert. I did the same.

La Verde. Centuries ago, there hadn't been any rain in La Verde. The aborigines left their dead to mummify in the dry heat.

When the weather changed and the rains came once a year, the land woke, the desert rolled with meadows, flowers burst from the dead soil, the air fluttered with butterflies and moths and bees. There were vineyards, tourists came for the rock formations and the hot salt caves, naturalists looked for spoor, hunters shot wildcats and pronghorn. Baths were dug near sinkholes where the mineral earth dissolved into reddish pools that tasted of iron and sweat and was supposed to be good for the skin, protecting it from the sun that poured death and sickness through the depleted skies.

But the rains came more frequently. And then it began to storm every night. During the day, the heat scorched everything, and at night, the rains taunted the desert to come to life. The aborigines could leave their dead elders propped against the stones, the paint on their lost ones' faces caking into red and white strips then crumbling into pink dust around gaping skulls. Now corpses were gone in a day, burnt then washed away. All the stories here led to ruin.

"Who are they?" Ishi whispered.

We were in the middle of a walk, before dawn but after the storm. People were hiking in the distance; we could see their lights flashing back and forth, a blinking shimmer on the horizon, the trek of disjointed stories across a dead land, movement in search of meaning where there was none.

"Sand widows," I guessed.

"What are they doing?"

"Looking for loved ones."

"What would be left?"

After the rains and the sun and the scorpions and the beetles?

"Nothing."

"Why do they do it?"

"Because that's what people do."

We spent a week in La Verde and saw nobody else.

Explorers and migrants still crawled out of the desert,

gasping for water in sand-bitten rags and a black cloak of flies. When their thirst was slaked, they talked only of their diminishment, their ordeals, how they survived by eating their dogs, their horses, or lizards sluggish in the dawn, how they guzzled whatever drops they could eke out of the miserly cactuses clustered in the pebbles, all thorn, no pulp.

They were the lucky ones. The rest died. They lay down and folded themselves up, a convenient package for death, pummeled by the rain and the heat into clay and sand, melting and leaving behind a few rings, a necklace, or some coins for the sand widows.

But the desert's history went back further than the aborigines and vineyards and mineral baths, past human history to primeval times when a giant roamed the earth. He bathed in the oceans, used hills for his pillows, and grazed on forests. He found this spot and curled up to take a nap. A horsefly, smaller than his smallest freckle, buzzed between his toes and stung him. The giant roared awake and hopped up and down, holding his stung foot and looking for the cause of his pain.

His hopping created the craters. His rage against the evil that the unseen can do made him take an enormous chisel to the earth, shearing off the top soil, shrubs, trees, and grasses, exposing a wounded red muscular layer beneath it, which dried and ossified in the sun. La Verde.

III.

The rains came on suddenly but we expected them. Every night they arrived, and when they hit it was fast and forceful like watching a stranger on the street swing at you in slow motion until right before impact when the punch speeds up into real time.

During the day, it was too hot to do anything but rest and sleep and peek out of the flaps at what was coming. Anything that lived in the desert spent the day hiding under pebbles, shale, shelves of rock, sleeping and sniffing the air, waiting for the storm to hit.

By midday, a bulk of clouds puffing with dark pride gathered over a ridge of mountains fifty miles of pale pearly desert away. Come mid-afternoon, the bucking cloudheads reared and rose over the mountains like horses reined in by the peaks. Sensing an unseen signal—a snap in the air, a rumble in the earth—the reins were let loose, and the cloud horses galloped, stumbling over the ridge, then rose into giants, hitching up the lowest black clouds like skirts and bolting across the desert, fabrics billowing. The storm raced with froth and spittle, splashing through the brown mist of rain at its ankles and the fractured twigs of lightening at its knees.

Ishi and I would be out by then, watching the storm bear down on us, until the forms melted into a shaggy black drape, sweeping in on us, absorbing the last of the sunlight. We ate supper, tinned fruit cubes in syrup and salty canned meat, as dusk collapsed with deliberate drama, sending up a shower of sparks across a sky slowly swallowed up by the curtains. The dark would settle, falling around us as if gravity had weakened and brought the night herself to earth.

This was the time of impatience. The world was in equilibrium. Between the stars and the storm, entirety balanced on a needle, the whole universe quivered and squeezed into a hum. It was heavenly. And it was possible to forget for a minute what was about to happen.

We didn't speak. I could smell the ozone of the coming

storm. Ishi's hair lifted into a black penumbra around her head. And at last, the rain came, fat pellets hurtling into the sand and sending up puffs of smoke. Each drop landed with a sigh. Then came the suddenness. The torrents hit.

Immediately wet, we held our faces up to the bolts of rain. Halos of blue light flowed around the tent poles. Ishi screamed. My ears and nose filled with rain, I would breathe the rain, not even sure what sounds I was making.

We bared our faces to the storm. We bared our chests. There was nobody to tell us what to do. Free and exposed, we held ourselves in the popping bulbs, wiping the rain out of our eyes and from around our mouths with wet hands and forearms. Half naked, we faced the worst and burst with laughter, great gales that had us swallowing rain, choking on the gusts of wind that would catch our open mouths and force a fistful of air down our throats.

When I couldn't take it anymore I reached around Ishi's shoulders and grabbed her, slippery as a fish, and pulled her into the tent like I was saving her from a train that hopped its rails. We tumbled through the flaps and collapsed on the folds of our sleeping bags, a velvety inch of cloth above the hard slate. We lay pale and chilled as goose-pimpled corpses, our chests heaving, arms angled around our heads, feet kicking in the storm, as the tent billowed and sucked blackly like we were inside a lung.

We were safe.

We survived.

After a few nights of plummeting through the storm it occurred to us to prepare a thermos of tea so that when we beat our retreat from the weather, it was there, toasty and kind to help us recover.

Bright blinks of lightening interrupted the dark, the rain bit at the canvas, the wind whipped the cords. We drank warm tea. The tent gasped, the storm hurled itself at us, the air was epileptic and electric, flashing white and black.

The storm thrashed for so long that I thought it would go on forever, that this is how we would die. Not from the trackers, not from the fate we knew was ours, but a death sentence in the storm.

And then I would hear Ishi breathing next to me, rustling on her sleeping bag. It was getting quieter. No longer trying to tear into us, the storm tapped the canvas, poked instead of punching, stroked instead of clawing. The rain came down in a soulful patter, seductive and constant. We rejoiced and felt loved and alive.

A few hours before dawn, the blowsy storm, tripped by the canyons in La Verde and slowed by its desert, stumbled like a drunk father into the distant sea. Rain drummed its fingers on the tent, slowly slowing. Spent, the air fidgeted. The tent flaps twitched. A blue snake of storm fire shimmered around the tent pole, clinging to it like a spirit pole dancer, then gave an impish kick and darted away.

That was our cue. We crawled out and watched the rear of the storm move into the last of the night.

Out in the open on the cool wet desert under a fresh-faced moon, there was too much to say but we thought that if only we started talking, we'd be able to say it all.

Ishi sipped her tea, toeing the mud. The ground was gashed with bow-shaped moats and oily slicks. By morning they would be gone, leaving only shadows across the sand.

And after the tea, we walked across the damp desert, stopping now and then to get our bearings, to watch the trek of sand widows with swinging torches, or just to look up at stationary stars and the forgotten satellites shooting one after the other in the storm-cleansed night.

There was too much to say but also nothing to say, and between the two only an ectoplasmic silence, globbed with sadness, happiness, fear and relief, our palpable if insensible way of saying goodbye to our lives. Because talking and words hadn't mattered at all.

IV.

We were given words, lots of them, as long as there was no writing. No books, no television, no newspapers, just talking. That was how we grew up. With language that disappeared as soon as we used it.

Ishi and I were from different residences. I was from a mansion built in a previous century. It stood at the head of a driveway lined by eight old elms, possibly the last, so thick and ancient that nothing could uproot them. The mansion's façade was red-faced and wide-eyed, like the squared head of a giant buried to its neck in the soil.

Ishi was from the west. Her residence was a pebbled cube of apartments around a courtyard domed by a curved sheet of sunglass. She said they could go into the courtyard and hang out there for as long as they liked, providing they didn't mind the green hue the sunglass gave everything.

As we approached the end, the residences were consolidated. We were the final group. We knew it was coming. The ones before us, who seemed so old but were not, had long gone, and even the ones who were only a year or two older had disappeared. They had somebody to look after. We had nobody. We were all cheated but the last of us were the most cheated, caught between nothing behind us and nothing ahead of us.

I don't know about the others, but for me life had been like getting a paper cut on a finger numbed by the cold: you could feel it but you couldn't; you were waiting for the pain but you knew you were protected from the pain as long as your finger was deadened with cold. As I got older and the residences got sparser, as stragglers came in from hundreds of miles away, I thawed and stung. The ranks thinned, a family gathering that got smaller every year. As love was beginning, love was ending.

And we panicked.

We fled. In twos and threes. We planned it over the course of an evening. Candles flickered on the tables and in the lit darkness we huddled and talked of places we had heard of: snow-fuzzed mountains; spewing volcanic landscapes with rusty pumice; the great wastelands with fraudulent Northern Lights.

I didn't choose to go with Ishi. She chose me. She only came up to my chest, a tomboy with black stubble across her scalp, and she spoke too much. I said nothing.

Nobody wanted La Verde. Two leaders from another residence had gone missing there. They were almost old, a boy and a girl. It scared us when we learned they had gone missing. But deep down we thought: they got away. They were still alive.

Ishi and I picked La Verde and a boy called Armond joked, "Going early, then?" but nobody cracked a smile. He knew how to recover though. "Maybe they'll find Tricia Lifton," he said, deadpan.

Even I giggled. It was hard not to mention Tricia Lifton without laughing. In a sealed-off space, we held an uncrushable locket close to our hearts: maybe Tricia Lifton would be there.

V.

I asked why Ishi had chosen me.

Because you're strong and quiet, she said.

"But why'd you agree?" she asked shyly.

I said, because you're the only one who knows what she's doing.

Later that night, I couldn't take it anymore.

"Ishi, wake up."

"What."

"You were crying again."

"No, I wasn't," she said, muzzy with sleep. "I don't remember dreaming anything sad."

"Ishi?"

"What."

"Do you cry in your sleep so you can pretend you don't know why you're crying?"

She turned away. Sunlight was glowing across the tent. Why did any of us cry when we slept? During the day, we were calm, but at night in the residences, you would hear only babbling.

She rolled over to face me, her mouth inches from my own. I could smell the faintly sour turn in her sweet breath, like crushed grapes that had been left out in the sun.

She said nothing until the silence burst and she couldn't stop herself. She asked me where Tricia Lifton was.

I told her I didn't know. None of us knew—before I finished, she said, "I'm going to find her."

She was disappointed by my silence. She didn't know I was choking on it.

"Tell me where she is," she whispered. "Again."

I took a breath.

"Nobody knows," I said, my breath mingling with hers. "There's the photograph from the Grassley meeting. It's just one shot of her looking upwards."

Ishi turned away impatiently. I was only saying what we always said when we met in private and discussed Tricia Lifton. I continued.

"Do you remember what she was wearing? A pink scarf. The ends dangle down the sides of her cheek. Her mouth is full. Maybe somebody just kissed her. A smile turns the corner of her lips. Is it coming on or fading?"

Ishi's hand reached out and took my own, like a cat's paw in mine.

"You describe it best," she said, "That's why I chose you. You know more words than anybody else." Embarrassed, she waited, then said, "Go on."

"She looks like summer. Not spring, not autumn, not winter. Summer." And then in a whisper, I said, "She didn't end."

Ishi cuddled close, nestling her head into my neck so I could smell the rain and the smoke from the campfire in her bristly hair. I knew she was asleep when she began to sob.

I was glad. I didn't want to know about her plans. And I wouldn't ask how she meant to find Tricia Lifton any more than I would ask her about her darkest fears.

A night later, we sat in the calm after the storm. We'd made a fire with twigs and rushes we'd kept in the tent. Ishi poked the flames with a branch whose end kept igniting in the blue heat over the coals. Rosewood, or blanched cottonwood, a sweet smoke curled up from the gray ring between the blackened branch and its red-hot tip. Ishi shook the flame out and then poked the stick in the embers and it re-ignited.

I could tell she was re-creating the image of a woman's face: a neck rising smoothly into jowls, downy cheeks, those famous vulpine eyes, the ceramic hair.

Ishi jabbed at the coals again, sending a waterfall of sparks tumbling over one another in their plummet to the sky.

"Would you tell me again?" she asked, shyly as if she asked me to kiss her. She stabbed the beating heart of the fire. The coals crumbled, and the fire gave a wave of its flickering paw and was sucked into the ash.

"The last picture we have is from the Grassley meeting. A rainy day. It shows her wearing a pink scarf. It comes down the sides of her face. She'd just untied it. She looks like she's about to greet somebody. She's not a child, she's a woman, a full-grown woman."

"How old is she now?" A typical question.

"She'd be in her forties." The standard answer.

She scowled at me. "I'm going to find her."

"'Stop saying that!"

"Why do you think I picked you?" Ishi threw the branch across the fire. "Together we could find her." The branch snapped into flames and a shower of sparks flooded up. "She's survived, we don't have to end—"

I jumped up and strode to the tent, baring my teeth.

"Don't you know who you are?" Ishi screamed at my back.

I spun back to face her. "I draw, that's who I am."

"And you believe that?"

"What else is there?"

Ishi said the words we couldn't even say to ourselves: "We don't have to disappear."

I wanted to scream. Nobody dared say that. We just laughed at the thought, we never said it. Steadying myself on the tent pole, I stared at her, unable to release the scream trapped in my chest. Even she was terrified. She pulled her knees up to her chest and stared at the embers, her lips trembling. By speaking those words, she had guaranteed they would never come true. Silence meant that we could hope. Not words. Silence. Being without words protected us from what would only come true if we put it into words. We laughed at the silence that came after her name because we all knew what was in it. But we never said it.

"Ishi."

It was her turn to stand. She faced me, lit from below like a demon.

"I'm the last," she said. "When I end, we're all gone. I'm going to find her." The way she said it, I believed her, but I said that I didn't. Without backing down, she went on. "I need you. I know your secret."

"How?"

A dozen satellites crossed the sky at once, a decrepit

convoy of shooting stars.

Ishi watched them fade. "Two years ago," she said, "a few of us slipped out one night and went to town. To spy on the people. But nobody was there anymore, they were all gone. We broke into a bar. It had a radio. We turned it on and listened to the music and then a man spoke. He was talking about how everything changed. Nothing we didn't know. But then he said that the only thing that was still true was that people know more about other people than they know about themselves." Ishi paused and looked down at the fire at her feet. "Look, Caye, I'm a counter—"

"I know."

"—but when I heard him, I stopped counting in my head. For the first time I can remember, I didn't think in numbers. Someone turned off the radio and the others talked about how people are different from us because they don't know themselves. We're different because we know ourselves, we don't have secrets from ourselves.

"But while the others were talking, I realized something. We had it all wrong. They know something about us we don't know." Ishi looked up at me. "Tricia Lifton was one of us and she survived. If we find her, we'll find the secret." She hunched against conspiracy. "That's why they don't want us to find her."

I didn't want to believe her but she said she knew my secret. Which one? It couldn't have been reading. If people found out I could read, it meant immediate death. That was the rule. But I hid it from the rest of us even more carefully than I hid it from people, because it was the rule that made us who we were.

"What comes after the end?" she said from the shadows. None of us asked that question but Ishi was willing to say things nobody else would.

I didn't know how to answer. We never had words for it.

"Caye, we'll find Tricia Lifton."

I went into tent and curled up. I don't know why, but I had a sudden desire to draw Ishi, the way the firelight licked her face. I had no paper and no pens and I fell asleep. When I woke up, Ishi was asleep next to me. She wasn't crying.

VI.

The next day we left La Verde. We had never been much good at planning for the future. We were out of rations, our packs were flaccid, no more water, tins of pears, meat.

We left the tent standing. Every few miles, we turned to look back. Absorbing the sun's rays, it glowed yellow as if lit from inside. Dusk fell and we could only look to where we thought the tent was, hoping a flash of lightening would illuminate it. It's hard leaving something you've lived in, even temporarily.

We were not so stupid to begin our walk in the middle of the day but we needed to leave enough time to beat the storm. We would know we were within a few hours' walk of the car when we heard the screech owls. They flapped into the desert from the fringe of trees lining the rio where they nested. The first hoot, Ishi and I jumped.

"First live thing that wasn't you," she said, putting an arm around my waist.

I cupped my hands and hooted, a reasonable enough impression. Ishi let me go. She was about to say something when we heard a far-off buzzing. It got louder. Soon, twin headlamps swept this way and that, going askew, even cross-eyed, before pointing at us.

"Searching for fugitives," I said.

Ishi shook her head and stuck out her chest as though the jeep was aiming straight for her and she was going to make the impact hurt.

She was right, they were coming straight at us. Ishi let her knapsack drop. I waited for instructions. They soon came.

"Put your stuff on the ground," said a voice distorted by a megaphone, "and put your arms up."

The jeep was far enough away that we could run for it but maybe they weren't alone. They might have trackers with them.

Two bright eyes focused on us. Moths flared like they were catching fire in the beams. We held our hands in the unsteady light. The jeep crawled towards us.

My arms went numb, my eyes tingled in the light until I closed them. When the jeep was a short distance away and the air was soggy and sweet with petroleum fumes, the mechanical voice addressed us again: "With your right hand, pull your shirt over your face." We followed the order. "Raise your hand again."

Our heads tucked into our t-shirts, I heard Ishi snort.

"Do they think this works?" she said, perfectly audible to me and to any sensors on the jeep's flanks.

"Quiet," I hissed. My face was getting hot under my t-shirt. I wanted to breathe air that didn't smell like my breath and underarms.

"This wouldn't save them if we were killers," she said, louder.

"Stop," I said. Ishi snorted again, this time directing her contempt towards me.

"Okay," said a man. Off the megaphone, his voice sounded smaller and fleshier. "You can take your heads out now."

Ishi yanked her shirt down. The headlamps were off but they had switched on a spotlight. Ishi snarled into the beam. From either side of the jeep hung a stetsons over a rifle, leftovers from when there were puma and wild goats to hunt. The spotlight crowded out anything else, but I knew they were alone. No trackers.

"What are you boys doing out here?" called the man leaning from the driver's seat.

Ishi bristled. "Boys?"

"Camping," I said.

"You sure?" said the other. His voice was plump and he spoke like he was making a joke. "Nobody but tickers camp out here."

He paused for laughter; when there was none, the pause became uncomfortable.

"Oh. Are you tickers?" he asked, swallowing the word like he was embarrassed even to say it.

"Hell yes, they are," said the other. The high beam was switched off and the two men hopped down, shadowy figures under the red echo of the extinguished spotlight.

22

They came up close, pointing rifles from their waists. One of them was tall and thin, the other short and heavy.

"You littler than I expected," said the thin one, eyeing Ishi up and down in the moonlight. "Not you," he said to me. "I expected all tickers to look like you."

"You're stupider than I expected," Ishi said.

The fat one nodded approvingly, like Ishi had performed a clever trick, and the thin one looked at us in contempt and bland wonder. His gun fell along his leg while he searched for something in his ear with his pinkie.

"We need to take you in," he said.

"Storm's almost here," the other added. "You didn't judge it right, being tourists and all. Better sit it out with us."

He was right. I could smell the change in the air. They waited for us to get into the back of their cruiser and then locked us in.

Ishi snuggled into the seat and immediately fell asleep. I hadn't realized how tired she was.

During the drive, the deputies glanced at us in the rear view mirror with a bemused curiosity that slowly turned to something else, something only perceptible in the way they glanced away from us.

VII.

"Grab a pew."

The fat deputy nodded at a wooden bench against the wall. The station was long and airless with slits for windows. A corrugated metal roof rattled as the rain smacked down. You could feel the wind push the station.

The bench had been defiled by etchings, carvings, and cryptic swirls in black marker. People had gouged the wood patiently but tenaciously with a fingernail or something sharp. I ran my finger over the grooves in the wood, smoothed by countless butts, and followed the curls, the trenches, the tentacles wrapping back on one another. I couldn't decipher the runes. Ishi put her head on my lap and began breathing heavily, shuddering now and then with a sob.

I tried to imagine the restless people who made the markings. Illegals, migrants, fugitives, militia, sand widows and survivalists, all the people who tumbled into these strange territories and collected in the rust pockets until they died or were found by the patrols, the ones who scrambled across the desert in search of peace, salvation, or their fortune only to end up lost and hot, clawing at their chests and hoping for death. They were incomprehensible, they were wildlife, the last things that weren't tamed. They left their mark with whatever they had because it mattered to them. It was no wonder their runes made no sense. They were barks in the wood, howls in ink. They were meaningless.

But I knew that wasn't true from the letters in the attic.

The letters. When I didn't hear from Teri, I'd go into my attic and pretend I was drawing. But I wasn't. I'd lock the door and remove the shoebox from the lowest shelf in an otherwise empty cabinet, and I'd read the letters over and over.

They never got old, just like me, just like the man who wrote them. Even when I thought I knew them from start to finish, I would come across new words, new stories, new emotions like they'd been put there since I last read them.

The letters were old, from a long time ago. He wrote of

leaving home and going to university, he wrote about his studies and enlisting in the military and getting the most glamorous uniform and going off to war, such a terrible adventure, and I felt like maybe I was in love.

But that wasn't why I kept reading them. What kept me going back had nothing to do with what I was feeling or what he was writing; it was the overpowering sense of having someone communicate with you. He knew that everything he wrote was understood by the aunt he greeted with confident affection, and through her, everything he wrote was understood by me.

I had one letter of my own and I kept it with the man's letters. When it was time to leave, it was the only one I brought.

I was soon scratching at a bare patch of wood with my fingernail.

Across from our bench was a trio of computer terminals and a braid of wires twined with black ties that led to the socket. A tracking satellite monitor and a radio system made an occasional fuzzy sound, a few sonic burps, then dimmed as if they were sick. There was a desk stacked with files. Buried behind it, where you expected chairs, were a pair of cots with sheets and blankets curled in human poses. On the far wall was a gun rack and behind our heads, a poster of a helium balloon ride over a desert, a different desert, one with yellow sands. The rest of the walls were empty wood panels. The place smelled like men.

Beside my thigh, using my fingernail, I put my initials into the wood. It felt good. Maybe that was it. Making your mark was the only difference between something and nothing.

The deputies changed out of their jeep gear, hanging up their stetsons, bug-eyed goggles, and tortoise-shell jackets.

The thin one came up to us, his lower lip thrust out in a pensive pout. He stood over us like a farmer who had just delivered mutant calves, wondering what to do with us and whether to kill us or let us live even though we disgusted and scared him. After a few seconds, he tapped Ishi like he wasn't sure if he wanted to interrogate her or see if she was alive. She was curled up. He gave her shoulder a push. She sat up and stuck her lower lip out just like his.

The deputy walked stiffly back to the table. Old injury, maybe. He fell into his seat behind the desk, checked a newspaper, then found a paper bag and removed a powdered doughnut. The sugar had caked into a crust along the bottom of the doughnut. Ishi and I watched as he distractedly broke it into three pieces and popped each one into his mouth, searching the walls for an image to anchor his thoughts.

After a week of canned vegetables and meat, the doughnut was the most appetizing thing I had ever seen. He didn't chew more than three times—I could sense Ishi counting—before he swallowed. He kissed each one of his fingers to get the last crumbs. I would have done it for him even though his fingers smelled like greasy hair because he hadn't showered in a few days and his head was getting itchy. I would have sucked the sugar out of his fingerprints. I wanted the morsel of doughnut lodged in the crease by his mouth, a sweet white fleck against the cracked corner where his lipless lips met.

The fat deputy saw me watching. He brought out a silvery tray with a torn doily and two broken doughnuts, one sugar, the other frosted chocolate.

Ishi shook her head. I took the chocolate one. The deputy swung the tray back in front of Ishi, giving her a second chance. She gave the world a thoughtful look, shrugged, and took it like she was doing him a favor. That made me want it. With a "well, you coulda had it" look she scarfed it down. The fat deputy laughed.

I nibbled my doughnut in an attempt to prolong the pleasure and then gave up any pretense and ate the rest in one bite. It was the most delicious thing I had ever tasted. Sweet stale pastry and chocolate, softened in the cabin's warmth. On the bottom, the chocolate was harder, coming off in flat chunks like slivers of sweet earthy almond.

"Want to lick the crumbs off the tray?" asked the fat deputy with a kind smile. "Cause if you don't, I will." I believed him. He held his weight in a languid way, a pink sling of puppy fat under his chin and a round belly straining the fabric of his shirt, pulling the buttons taut.

The other seemed unsure what to do with his body. On his forearms, murky tattoos melted bluely into his skin. His thin neck was like the trunk of a birch tree coiled with the shadows of ivy tendrils.

"How old are you?" asked the fat one. Ishi was watching the other, who looked straight back in a dull-eyed way. Fatigue collecting in the puffiness around his eyes. I interrupted before Ishi could answer.

"We're registered."

The fat deputy shrugged. The thin one looked at us with bored resignation.

"Computer's down," he said. "We have to wait until the storm is over."

Ishi couldn't keep quiet. "I'm seventeen years, four months, three days, and nine hours."

The fat deputy slapped the table. "Did you see that? He's a counter."

"She," corrected Ishi, folding her arms tightly.

"A 'she' counter?" said the fat deputy, incredulous, reaching out to tap his partner, who leaned out of the way and busied himself with unlacing his boots.

"There were over a thousand of us," said Ishi.

"I never seen one of you before," said the fat deputy, shaking his head at the mystery of it, "let alone a counter."

Ishi shot him a look that would curdle milk.

The thin deputy dropped his laces, agitated. "I can't tell how old you are."

"Cut me in two," snarled Ishi, "and count the rings."

"You make me sick."

"One year!" screamed Ishi. "You have one year left to live."

The thin deputy fell back, his face ashen. I looked at his feet to see if someone had uncorked him and let all the blood drain out. He wiped his mouth against the back of his wrist and began to tremble.

"I got a baby," he said. "A girl."

The fat deputy inched over to the weapons cabinet,

feeling for the guns. They looked scared. Nobody returned my smile.

The thin one, shaky and pale, was the most dangerous.

"Deputy Meyers," I said quietly to him, "Don't—"

"How'd you know my name?" he shrieked.

"You called each other by name," I answered.

"I don't remember him saying my name," he stammered, a hand over his badge. "Noah, did you call me by my name?"

"Might have," said Noah, unsure; and then just as unsure: "They can't read. How could he know? I mean she, or whatever it is. They can't read."

Ishi shot me a look as well. Meyers was working his pistol out, his finger slipping through the trigger guard.

"If this 'un can read—"

The door crashed open. Wind blasted in and everybody blinked. Meyers yanked at his pistol. Noah grappled with the gun rack.

A tall man in a stetson and rain-lashed poncho bundled in and closed the door. He was huge, filling the doorway, but he was also relaxed, in rain-polished black leather boots, jeans, and, under the poncho he hung on a hook by the door, a hunting jacket. His goggles were around his neck. No bullet-proof vest. He peeled off his gloves and slapped them against his thigh.

"Chief," said Noah, relieved and embarrassed.

"What do we have here?" he asked, inspecting Ishi and me. A white-toothed grin, like a calcified crack, opened up in his granite features.

Noah took a deep breath and explained. Eventually the chief held up a hand.

"Holster the cannons," he instructed. "Don't want anybody wasting a ticker in here. They got trackers to deal with them."

"That one said Meyers was gonna die—"

"I heard enough." He shook his head sagely. "They're not prophets, they can't read, but they are sharp as hell. It's most likely that the boy— "

"Girl," hissed Ishi.

"—is working you up, and this other one did hear Noah address you by name. Now, what'd I say? At ease, boys."

Meyers slipped his pistol into his belt. Noah's hand dropped from the gun rack. Nobody was convinced of anything other than the possibility of murder. Ishi decided to be friendly. She scrunched her neck down in a little girl shrug.

The chief's grin disappeared and he tossed his gloves on the table. The man knew what he was doing. He had no interest in pleasantries unless they served a purpose. The friendly tone and big ole grin were just tactical, to get his frightened men to put away their guns.

All business now, he sniffed. "Why'd you call me in for a couple of tickers?"

"Computer's down," said Noah.

The chief came over. "They been fed? They look hungry. And old for tickers. They're the last ones." He gestured at us like we were specimens. "They cause anybody any trouble other than laying a hex on you, Meyers?"

Mumbled no's.

"You're one of the last counters," said the chief to Ishi.

Ishi's nod was barely perceptible, not much more than a downward glance.

"Boys, do you know what this little girl can do? She can sit at a terminal for days without stopping, calculating as fast as a computer, making those red marks—"

"Chips," said Ishi, bored.

"Boys, a 'chip' is when she makes an assumption. I read about this in the papers. Tell me if I'm wrong, girl. Every algorithm has its forks, right? The computer can take both forks but a human can only take one. She makes a red hash mark when she makes an assumption, goes a certain way with a calculation. It's a way of thinking I cannot fathom. Like they got baubles for brains, all crystal-clear inside those skulls. I simply don't understand them."

"Me either," I chimed in. I had no facility with their system, their marks, their chips.

The chief looked at me hard. "That's right, you don't look

like a counter."

Ishi stiffened. "What do counters look like?"

"I don't know," said the chief, "but this one looks like—"

"An illustrator," Ishi said.

"What do you illustrate?" asked the chief.

My hand sucked in my stray thumb. I had been scratching at the wood. The chief looked at the bench. I shifted to cover the marks, relaxed my hands, and said, "I do drawings and watercolors."

"No way."

"That's what I do."

"You're not a killer?"

There was a rumor that some of us were killers. The counters had been selected for their mathematical gyri. Even when the runt embryos were removed, they were smaller. Others were selected for a variety of things, mostly scholar-athletes. But there was a rumor that some had been selected for military purposes, cell lines developed not in Orange County or Delhi but at an airbase, cell lines cultivated, prepped, and developed into murderous embryos, strangler infants, deadly toddlers, and finally assassin teenagers who could take out a brigade with their bare hands. There were comic books about killers who went on rampages and hid out in ruins and launched attacks until they were hunted down by a tracker who'd lost his family to a rogue killer. The trackers were the heroes.

Rumor had it that the killers had incredible physical prowess. It was never consolidated like a superhero's. It was a blend of barely noticeable things: heightened senses, a precision of movement that let them run along a taut wire, the strength and agility to learn new fighting skills in a matter of minutes. What was really frightening about killers was that they were supposed to be impervious to pain. And they wouldn't stop until they were killed or bundled in ropes and tossed into a cage where they would thrash until they lost consciousness and were finished off with a cut to the throat.

But then nobody was sure if they existed.

"I'm not a killer," I said, perfectly happy to leave it as a possibility. Ishi shifted up against me.

The chief was tracing a finger up and down her thigh. She walleyed him. He stopped. Adjusted his belt. Belched.

"Run them through the system in the morning. If there's a problem, let me know. If not, let them go."

I would like to say that we killed them.

How would we have done it?

Meyers was the one on the edge. He had been subsisting on doughnuts and he was tired and lonely, unable to sleep at work where he was unliked or at home where his wife curled as far away from him as she could and his daughter woke up toothless and bawling every two hours. A lousy father. He was primed to go off.

I would tell him Ishi was right, that he had only a year left and I'd look at Noah and laugh. Because Noah was stupid and couldn't tell the difference between a joke and a confession, he would laugh too. That would make Meyers furious. He was scared of us but he hated people more because he was one of them. The ones who acted like they hated us the most were like that. We were the excuse for people who hated other people but didn't know where to put their hate.

Meyers wouldn't know whether to shoot Noah before shooting us but that would be enough. Get it just right, make two weak men who hate the weakness they see reflected in the other realize they were going to get a shot at each other, and they shoot, Meyers an instant before Noah but not fast enough. Two shots, two down.

And the chief? He was something else. He had charisma and power. He knew how to manage their hate and fear but he wouldn't know what to do when they were lost to hate and fear.

Ishi could get to him while he watched his boys shoot each other. She was like that. Small-boned, wriggly, like a broken spider stripped of four limbs, Ishi could get any bully just by scrunching up her face like a victim about to turn the tables, with a defiant kink in her neck, a scowl.

I'd begin chanting nonsense, scat, old rhymes we had learned about hate, fires, flowers torn from the ground, car crashes, scalding tea; I'd mix in their names and anything else I could see. It's an eerie sound, as random and scrawling as the etchings on the bench, because when we chant, we chant like we did when we were three or four, using screechy falsettos that are nothing like a child's sweet pipes.

The chief would be confused, he'd fall under Ishi's attack like a bull under a jaguar, and I'd join in. Ishi, the sweet-breathed counter, and me, the giant illustrator who didn't care about anything, laying into a chief next to his self-murdered deputies. It would be easy. Then we'd lay off.

"Chief," I'd say, "Why don't you go to that gun rack and select a rifle. You'll be using it on yourself, so choose carefully."

He would do as I say, following my instructions with heaviness in his limbs as if his muscles were filled with iron ore, but with a terrified brightness in his eyes.

"Good. Open wide. Put the gun in. Now pull the trigger."

But we didn't. Noah drifted from the gun rack and slumped against the computer terminal. Meyers sat on the cot to remove his socks, peeling them off one by one, snapping the smell of sweet feet across the room.

I did ask the chief a question, though.

"Chief, have you ever seen a ticker before?"

"I said I hadn't."

"That's what I thought. You'll never see us again."

He nodded slowly. "I know that."

He stopped at the door and seemed to be thinking. The way he held the brim of his hat, like it was a napkin he was about to lay across a dead relative's face, was delicate, almost caring. When he turned to look at me, he didn't seem so cruel. "That's a strange certainty, ain't it?" he said, then he put his hat on and left into the storm.

VIII.

After the chief was gone, Noah and Meyers slipped into the room's shadows until their shift was over. At dawn, they prepared for their departure with languid yawns that began as deep breaths, drifted into melodic ahs, and ended on flat sighs.

Neither introduced us to the two grizzled men who replaced them. They came in without a word, responding to the nods of the departing deputies with tiny jerks of their heads. The newcomers gave us a quick once-over, no more than that. One opened up a box of pastries, took a bread roll, and passed the box to the other. After eating, they settled in their chairs and played games in the newspapers.

The computer system had been re-booted but the two men did nothing about us.

Ishi and I ignored Noah and Meyers when they returned even though we were glad to see them. With our arms crossed like petulant children, we sat on the wooden bench, thanklessly drank mugs of tea and ate more doughnuts.

Noah sat at the bank of computers. He typed, read something, glanced up, then took Meyers to the gun rack. They spoke into their hands with their backs to us. I could make out a few words. "Last ones." That was no surprise. "Trackers." That too. But then I thought I heard Meyers say "Tricia Lifton." I gasped. The deputies stiffened. I coughed like I had an itch in my throat.

And then Noah gave us permission to go. There was no ceremony, no apology, nothing but Noah's wobbling "on your way" and the wan expression of Meyers.

At the door, Ishi turned. "Hey idiots, how do we get to our car?"

Noah drove us to the parking lot. The car was grimy and someone had tampered with the tires but it started.

The car hopped out of the parking lot and we drove fast. We passed Noah in his jeep and he gave us a wave without looking, like he didn't know us.

For the first hundred miles, Ishi took the wheel and I

folded myself in the passenger seat. The road was straight and slick with the night's storm steaming off the tarmac. Every dip saw us rushing through a puddle of hot fog like a maddened frog with its backside burning blue.

Eventually the road lifted from the desert and we crested ridges, soaring over a black landscape under a cloudless night; we were moving through the emptinesses of space, filled or not, arbitrarily, with no design. The headlamps reflected on the sheen. Ishi turned off the lights and we drove by the light of the moon. When only contours are visible, a journey is much smoother.

Dawn came on like a disease. We could sense it long before we could see it, a suggestion of queasy light, the hint of a halo above mountains. If you looked directly at the peaks you could see nothing, but if you looked out of the side of your eye you could perceive a glowing mistiness. And then the sun struck, a fire along a serrated knife-edge.

We were making good time but had nowhere to go. Ishi wanted to say something but I was enjoying the silence. She was plotting. She hadn't given up on including me in her plans. The highway came down into foothills, then churned through fields of soy, rape, and corn, past farms where lights were already on in the kitchens and tractors had been driven out of their barns. Later, I was behind the wheel and Ishi was asleep in the backseat.

I focused on the rumble of the engine. The air was cooler and I rolled down the window. It woke Ishi.

"Where are we?" She crawled up next to me. "Was I asleep for long?"

I shrugged.

"You know what I was dreaming about?" she asked, cracking open a can of juice and taking a sip, then getting all excited. "Children. Getting off an elevator. I was watching them do it. Have you been in an elevator?"

I hadn't.

"Do you think kids, the first time they're in an elevator, freak out when the door closes and then opens and they're somewhere else?"

"No," I said. "They just understand."

"How? It's not instinctual, it's not genetic, it's not like we've been going up and down on elevators for thousands of years."

"They sense the movement."

"It's too subtle," she said sharply, with more anger than I expected, like I was ruining her dream. "I'll bet you can't tell if you're going up or down. You know what I think?"

"What?"

"They don't care. You can't be freaked out if you don't care. Kids accept the world as a place where some things don't have explanations. That's like us."

"Having no explanations?"

"No, we just get into life and then get off."

She crushed the can and set herself in the seat so she was facing forward.

"I'm not going to do nothing until it's time to get off, Caye. We're going to push a button."

I didn't want to keep the conversation going. The button was already pushed. Any moment, the doors were going to open wherever we were and we were going to step out and end. But I didn't say that. Instead I said, "It's your dream."

Ishi grabbed my hand and seemed really happy.

"It's not just mine. You've dreamed it too."

I hadn't.

But then it came on: a belief. All Ishi was asking was for me to believe. And suddenly I did.

We didn't stop holding hands until we reached the outskirts of a city, crushed and gray, busy but lifeless. The traffic lights blinked red, yellow, and green, semaphores for a broken robot.

A cruiser pulled out as soon as we hit the city limits and followed us for a few miles. I couldn't see through the windscreen. Eventually, it turned and trailed away, satisfied of something. A truck with a tinted windscreen replaced it, bumping behind us, turning when we turned.

We cut through the city center.

"Trackers?"

Ishi turned to look back. "I don't think so," she said. She scrunched up her nose. "No, I've changed my mind. They're trackers."

At an intersection, the stoplights flickered to solid red.

"Go for it," said Ishi, hurriedly.

"Are you sure?"

"Go for it!" she screamed.

I revved up then slammed the brakes. I should have listened to Ishi. The flatbed rammed us from behind.

The jolt pushed us into the intersection. A truck crashed into us with the loud slap of metal on metal. We were pushed sideways and pinned between the truck's broken face and a lamppost elbowing through Ishi's window.

The car filled with steam. Ishi had a cut on her forehead over a lump that grew as big as one of her fists. The cut barely bled but Ishi was pale. She made a face like she was about to throw up. I couldn't feel any of my body: I knew it was there and I knew there was something called pain in my arm but I knew that if I didn't look I wouldn't feel it.

"Are you okay?" I asked.

Ishi, white-lipped, didn't say anything. There were no more windows on my side of the car, only the grille of the truck inches from my face. My arm was damp with blood and dusted with a silvery powder, the shattered glass. The air was sharp with oil and the acid of brake fluid.

Ishi was holding my good hand.

"I said 'go'" she whispered. "You shouldn't have stopped." And then: "Go find Tricia Lifton." She was looking at me sadly, then gulping like she was swallowing back vomit.

Sirens and flashing lights. I felt a stiffness in my neck and the tingle of sharp needles in my arm. I couldn't bear to look at Ishi.

"Find her," she said.

A paramedic clambered onto the front of the car. He signaled for me to look him straight in the eye and then made turning motions with his right hand. I turned the ignition off. It was suddenly very quiet. He signaled okay.

"Help us," I whispered.

Someone came up beside him and said something. They slid away.

"Help us?"

He was gone. People came to look but were held back by men in leather jackets. And then something was thrown over the windshield. A fire cloth, cutting out the light. Ishi took short breaths without an audible exhalation. It sounded like someone was making love to her.

They were waiting for us to die.

I watched as Ishi's face slowly relaxed, the look of pained concentration melted into an open-mouthed sleep. A moment later, there were no more breaths.

"You're not crying, Ishi," I said. Her hand was limp in mine.

IX.

Nick hustled into the car, slamming the door and planting his feet hard under the dashboard. A blast of air accompanied him, a cold bullying ghost charging in after him. Even once the gulp of frozen air dissipated into the breathy warmth of the car's interior, a chill came off Nick, another ghost fleeing his body. He was breathing heavily and clamped his hands under his armpits. He could barely suppress a smile.

"Let's go," he said. The smile he was holding back snapped across his face and he beamed. I didn't know what it meant. He was a nice-looking guy who was always smiling; when you asked him what he was smiling about, he'd just broaden his smile and say, "I don't know," as if it was an answer. You never got the sense that something secret or funny was going through his head, just that he'd rather be smiling than doing anything else.

The building where he had been holing up was the only one on the street that wasn't brick. Its aluminum siding was dented, creamy icicles hung from gutters, coils of telecommunication wires formed tangled nests on the corners. The wires looped to nearby poles, giving the impression that they kept the house from toppling over.

I never saw anybody else living there but Nick assured me he didn't have the building to himself. He had been occupying one room on the second floor. After a week or two, he'd brought up a mattress, chairs, and a television. No table, no drawers, no shelves. He kept his clothes in a box and used a neighbor's bathroom. He brought girls from the bars and enjoyed the sex. I imagined him waiting alone in that room for most of the week, smiling to himself.

The box, the mattress, the television, he left behind. He inspected his clothes, carefully folded some into a plastic bag, and then tossed the rest into the dumpster in the alley. We were about to drive away when he told me to wait, mumbled about a floorboard, and raced back.

I felt a surge of panic. If we could find each other, the

trackers could find us.

But nothing happened. He came back and flashed the dull barrel of a pistol tucked in the crotch of his armpit.

"Adios," he said, as we drove away. I guess if you're happy, saying goodbye isn't that hard.

The streets were empty. There was nobody about. Nick told me about the people he'd met. I don't know how he got so comfortable with them. He didn't act like they were our enemies. Another reason to be happy, I suppose.

"I was waiting for you," he said, looking out the window.

We followed an underpass onto the highway ramp. In a slice of no-man's land was a fallen bollard and an uncoiling spool of razor wire, like an acid rain-melted sculpture of a man, the razor wire stinging insects, metal tracing their orbits.

Nick followed my gaze and furrowed his brow like he was thinking of something bad, then the smile came back. "Terrible world, isn't it?"

It was. I couldn't say it. I couldn't even think it. He saw me struggle with the thought and laughed. I couldn't find anything funny in it. I was losing words. Just blank spaces where words should be, like the emptiness in the back seat where Ishi should have been. Nick must have been full of similar emptinesses. He was also living in a world where everyone we knew had disappeared forever, where we became friends with people we couldn't trust, shacked up with people we couldn't love, made plans with people with whom we had no future. Nick filled the emptiness with smiles like they were cups of warm tea from a never-empty teapot. Nothing could fill that emptiness for me, not even Ishi's ghost leaving an indentation in the back seat. The car was getting hot. I cracked a window. Frigid air whined in.

We went to the town center. The only cars we saw were leaving, their windshield wipers beating back and forth. We passed a truck, screaming in lower gears, burning transmission fluid.

"You're always so quiet," Nick said and smiled like it was a good thing.

When I didn't say anything, he smiled again. The

downtown buildings were a dark gray mass. The drizzle turned to snow.

"How's your arm?" He touched my shoulder, curious. "I'll bet they didn't expect you to leave the hospital."

He laughed. He didn't know what to make of it. Maybe that was it. Maybe he was just filling the emptiness with the burr of confusion, which came out as a laugh. My arm was tingling.

When the ambulance arrived at the hospital, the paramedics got out to get the doctors. They didn't hurry. They didn't expect me to survive the crash, they didn't expect me to survive the ambulance ride, there was no way I would survive the night. While they were in the emergency room, I unbuckled myself from the stretcher and slipped out the side door. I didn't wait to see the look of surprise on their faces when they came back and I was gone.

The snow was melting on our windshield but collecting in furrows along the side of the road. Nick fell asleep. The wind whipped the snow into curlicues that snaked alongside us.

The storm worsened into a blizzard.

The last time I had seen such a hard snowfall was at a fair. We were invited to go the day after it officially closed. We were given candy floss and free rides on the carousel until the snow hit and everything came to a halt. The air was whipped and white. We made snowballs and threw them at the people cowering under makeshift shelters and blue tarpaulins strung between stalls, lashed to foot-long iron spikes jackhammered into the soil.

The people who had been giving us sweets and free rides turned their bodies to absorb the blows of our snowballs. They tucked their chins in. We laughed and pounded our hands against our thighs to keep them from freezing as we scooped up more snow, compacted it into icy balls with clods of dirt and stray blades of grass, and hurled them, following each impact with a loud cheer and upraised arms.

One of the roundabouts fired a pistol; after the crack and the whistle of a bullet, hot in the cold air, we raced away, slapping our buttocks as we zigzagged off. Maybe we were children, I thought.

The downtown was empty. Business centers were locked, restaurants closed, shops bolted in a quilt of chain link. A monorail buzzed overhead. Nick woke up.

"Left here," he said.

We pulled in front of Eagle Bank, next to a squat and tired liquor store. The sign was still up but the bulbs had been removed, leaving an exoskeleton of fading colors.

I turned the engine off. Nick took the pistol.

"It's best if I do this alone," he said, "so things don't get out of hand."

He opened the door, got out, and let it shut, leaving in the car a groping cold bulk of air in his shape.

A pair of surveillance cameras leaned out from the liquor store. One was moving, whirring its eye up and down and to the left and right, as if following a child in a playground. Its twin, pitted against the alley, was cocked to one side, not quite dead, but broken as if it had just been told that somebody died.

I waited. I was doing everything I could to avoid looking for Nick between each beat of the wipers. The Eagle Bank was brick with a white classical portico, incongruous in its dignity from the rundown, beat-up buildings around it. The handicap access ramp seemed preserved from an earlier time, with a bent iron rail and a cracked concrete base, spouting dead weeds and a trim of hard yellowed grasses collecting snow.

A man left the bank, holding his jacket close. He curled suspiciously over the iron rail. A tracker? I clenched my fists in my lap and stared ahead, watching him out of the side of my eyes. He came down the steps, approached the car. I used my thumb to crack my fingers, one by one. Staggering as if drunk, bullied by the wind, he turned and leaned heavily into the snows. I shook out the tension in my hands.

I had been told that it was okay to be nervous on your first heist. Nick told me. It was also his first heist.

But I wasn't nervous and that was what worried him.

I heard hollow stuttered taps.

Nick bustled out of the bank and tumbled into the car in a

metallic shower of snow.

As soon as he closed the door, I pulled out and turned under the monorail struts. No sirens, no police cars, no trucks. Just Nick, breathing. He smelled like metal.

"What happened?"

I turned north, allowing the storm to push us from behind, feeling the car tense and relax in the winds. Nick said nothing. We drove between big glass buildings whirling and hiding in the blizzard like children playing in the snow.

"How much did we get?"

He gave me a scared look. I thought he was going to kill me. It made sense. Keep whatever he got and enjoy himself before the end or whatever. Or maybe he wasn't one of us. Trackers knew how to get our guards down.

I asked him again. "How much did we get?"

Chunks of snow plopped against the windscreen.

"Is anybody dead?" I asked.

"I didn't wait to find out."

I asked a third time. "How much did we get?"

Nick shook his head and this time, he wasn't smiling. But I was. Truth was, we were all idiots.

A little while later, Nick got out of the car and bought a cup of tea with the loose change in his pocket. He spent the last money we had on the cup of tea, which we shared, taking careful little sips.

X.

We had no idea how much time was left but when I mentioned Tricia Lifton, Nick sighed with relief like he had been harboring a secret that was finally out in the open. I had to laugh. If ever there was someone who didn't seem to be bottling anything up, it was Nick.

Now he got excited.

"They know where she is," he said excitedly, as if they were hiding a present from us.

"Did you ask?"

"Who?"

"Your lovers?"

He frowned like he hadn't even thought of it. "The time never seemed right," he said. A better excuse than admitting he hadn't considered it. "Do you know anyone we can ask?"

I nodded. Yes, I did. Nick didn't ask who. We left the heartland and headed towards the coast.

Windmills chopped the air over refineries like discarded engines with dusty blocks and sooty cylinders. We camped by the side of the road. I slept in the backseat, trying not to think about where we were going. Nick slept under the car. When he woke up, the left side of his face was red and pitted from the gravel.

Finally, we pulled up in front of the house. I recognized it from the blotchy black-and-white picture that came in the letter. But it was painted lime-green, much brighter than I expected.

The houses on either side looked like they were the ones cut out from a dirty newspaper. Lawns were stippled brown as if a giant had splashed acid across them and windows were boarded up or sealed over with plastic and a blue duct-taped cross.

The house was overabundant with life. The window sills drooled ivy, a bougainvillea eked its way up the door jambs, magenta bracts drooping over the doorway like skeletal hands showering petals, a freeze-frame of purple confetti tossed over those entering or leaving. Ferns, dense and broad-leaved, fanned out along the path. In the middle of a lawn was a rock garden hugged by dark green succulents, and just beyond it, a herb garden bursting with tangy bushes buzzing with pebble-sized bees and the bumbling inefficiency of cream-winged butterflies.

I couldn't get out of the car, it was too much. Nobody could understand. Not Nick, not Ishi, none of the ones I grew up with.

I stared at the blooms and the lime-green house, and everything was extinguished in me, washed out, suds and all. Just a tickle in my gut, and my foot tapping of its own accord to a stutter inside me.

"Wouldn't want to have lived here," said Nick. He was being kind.

I wasn't surprised. He was a nice guy. But then, I was surprised: for all we knew we were the last two. What was the point in being nice anymore?

"Do it," grunted Nick, letting his nerves show.

I shook my head, not so sure.

"They'll know, won't they?" he said.

Hope is a touching thing.

I got out, taking his pistol. I felt a tinge of nausea, drew a few breaths of the cabbagey air, and then walked up the path, each step accompanied by a question: was this familiar? Was this or this or this?

No. It wasn't.

Even if the people were connected to me, there would be no reason for me to have been here. We were taken away immediately.

Or so we were told. Maybe I was here for a year or two? Did I learn to walk here? Was there something here that explained who I was? I'd wondered what the people passed down to me that couldn't be listed on a form, the unintended similarities, the accidents that became the better part of who I was.

And what about the things I'd done? Did they pass on artistic skills by mistake or was that something they selected for, giving each other loving looks and cooing as they chose the color

44

of my hair, my eyes?

I drifted up a path nowhere to be found in my memories, trapped in a turbid silence that expanded, pushing away the birds, the wind, the wind chimes. The bees and the butterflies fled. Something stabbed my ankle. A fibrous blade of grass, broken along its stem. I wondered if Nick, Ishi and the others were filled with this much nothing. Who would have known what it was like to walk up this path? Maybe the man who wrote the letters and longed to return home. Maybe the letters stopped because he came home? Somehow I knew otherwise.

My first memory, what was it? A snapshot. An edge of light that broadened. A hot orange blur is next. Not a real memory. Then after that, a real memory for sure, of a pitch black night, a white blaze where the house was, red spinning lights, sirens that silenced when the fire engines arrived, and the peculiar feeling of my front being warmed by the fire while my back was chilled. Fourteen of us died. We always knew it was arson but nothing happened. We moved to the old mansion.

A few more steps. I searched for another memory, an excuse to pause, but nothing came.

Had I not seen the cat in the windowsill, I would have turned around and left. Nick would have something stupid to say but I'd ignore him and we'd leave, banging against the cars left for dead along the sides of the road.

The cat was a silky little thing. It couldn't have been more than a year or two old, its sharp tail pointed up, back arched, its paws splayed. After stretching, it looked at me knowingly. Yes, it said, you're the one we've been waiting for.

I wanted to ask, How could the people raise you after what they did? What right did they have to take so perfect and precious a creature and lock it in their home, forcing it to pay homage to their shins for a meal?

I pressed the doorbell. The cat dropped from the inside ledge.

A few moments later, a man opened the door.

He had droopy eyelids and bags under his eyes, giving him a look of fatal boredom. Wisps of white hair curled around his ears, which were large and floppy with still-detectable points in the lobes where they had been pierced many years ago. The mouth was heavy, and a tongue emerged to dampen his lips. He did not see very well. He held the door open and steadied himself against the wall.

"Hello," I said.

After a moment, he raised his eyebrows. The hand fell to his side and he teetered.

I walked past him and in. The hall was musty, dim, saturated with an internal fog that made the air damp, too alive to be healthy. A mantle was piled with letters, keys, buttons, coins, a book of matches, whatever was in his pockets as he shuffled in or out. He led me to a room with overstuffed chairs, a sofa, and a table with books and an empty picture frame. The shelves held decorative glass bottles, jugs, pots with cacti and geraniums.

"Do you know who I am?" I asked.

"Your mother died a month ago."

"Oh."

There would be no rush into her arms, no apology, I would not be hugged by her and forgiven. Did I feel cheated? Relieved? Or nothing at all?

"Tea?" he asked.

"Yes, please."

He had been a painter, he said.

"Do you want to see one of my works?"

I shook my head no, but he didn't see.

He left me alone then returned with a square canvas and showed it to me. Dark blue oil with a black square barely visible in the middle.

The more I looked, the less certain I was of the black square. It might have been a trick of the light and the pattern of the strokes.

But the more I looked, the more colors I saw. There was a thread-thin streak of white, which, picking up traces of the blue, became sky-blue. A spot of yellow under a spot of green under a spot of red. The etiolated suggestion of a traffic light?

I turned it around. He had painted his name on the back—Alistair Mallory.

"It's nice," I said, handing it back. I wanted to hold it longer but to do so would be to concede something.

He placed it carelessly on the table.

"Can you imagine what it's like to hate your child?" he asked, not unkindly.

"I can't have one."

"No, you can't," he said.

Can't have a child or can't imagine what it's like to hate your child? Either way, he went on, "I wanted to love you. It was all your mother and I wanted. You were helpless and despite it, we wanted to keep you."

"Despite what?"

"Despite what you are."

"This?" I pointed to myself.

"Have you seen yourself?"

"Yes."

"Well, then. Your mother was a very good person." He looked away. Bored? Scared? Old?

I cleared my throat. "Will you tell me where she is?"

"Your mother? I told you she passed."

I laughed. I had already forgotten her. "No," I said, "Tricia Lifton."

His eyes glazed over. I was no longer his child. I was one of us again.

"No."

I put the cup of tea down and was about to stand. But there was another question, one I hadn't told Nick about.

"Can I ask you something else?"

"You might as well."

"Why did you write the letter?"

He turned away, holding a finger in the air as if conducting a tune I could not hear. "A father's mistake. Curious you should know about it."

"I still have it." I removed it from my pocket and held it out.

"Then it's good you can't read, you've spared us an awkward moment."

"I can read."

"No you can't, it's impossible." His hand dropped from the air and he turned, perplexed. "They said you'd never learn."

"I learned slowly from the envelopes I was given and letters I found. It's a code. Once you know it, you can read anything."

His mouth opened in a silent laugh as if he was impressed, then snapped shut. He brushed his stomach and snorted. "You're lying," he sighed with a paternal disappointment.

I reached for one of the paperbacks on the table, opened it in the middle, and read the first line I saw: "She's dying to meet you." I held the book out with a finger pointing to the sentence. "Do I need to go on?"

He allowed bemusement to cross his face, like I'd performed a clever trick but didn't even know how clever it was.

"You have your mother's eyes. Don't you want to ask about her?"

It was a good question; the answer was no. At most, she was somebody who was looking over his shoulder as he wrote the letter.

"I'm an artist, too," I said.

"Your mother had a wonderful eye."

"Were you selecting for it?"

"You don't know the truth, do you?"

I said nothing.

"Any artistic abilities may be genetic or not, but they are entirely accidental. You were not bred for them, I can assure you of that. And I know all about your art. Your mother met that woman, Teri, and they decided to make something of you, something you're not. An artist? No, you are not an artist, you are a monster, an illiterate monster even if you think you can read."

"Then why'd you write the letter?"

He sat down and took his cup of tea.

"You see, that's just it, you would never understood. That's why you're illiterate, functionally illiterate. My letter was a way of speaking to the child I never had by sending a letter to the child I did, knowing it would never read the damn thing."

In the chair, he shriveled, his clothes hung loosely around his frame. He was becoming smaller by the minute, shrinking before my eyes like a fast-forwarded film of a flower desiccating and dying.

"You and I both know who you really are and, letter or not, the truth will come out."

He was right. The truth does come out; it comes popping out of the elevator like a group of children who couldn't care less how they got somewhere different. I wasn't coming for information about Tricia Lifton, an apology, an explanation or a reunion.

He sipped his tea, kissing the rim of the china cup without taking his eyes from me. I removed Nick's pistol from my pocket, aimed, and shot him in the forehead, fast enough that he couldn't say anything.

His head flicked back and then forward and he followed it, tipping out of the seat. The cup rolled out of his hand, hit the floor, and bounced once with a splash. It did not break until he toppled onto it, crunching it beneath his frail chest. The cat shot out of the room, scrabbling to turn the corner at the door.

I pulled the letter out from my pocket and stood over him.

"Dear child," I read, "You have no idea what it is like to have brought something like you into the world. Who does one loathe? Oneself? Your mother? You? Your mother cannot even look at you but I held you in my arms and searched your face. May you never know what it is like to look at something so fragile, so desperate for love, and to see the monster in it. I wouldn't wish that on my worst enemy. A.M."

In the hallway, I took the book of matches from the mantle. A smooth orange wave burned across the letter. When it was a curling black shadow, I crushed it into ash.

A smudge of gray welled up and seeped through the

windows and the lime-green house gave way to flames. Heat shimmered across the garden. The cat darted into the garden, as the first dull thud of an explosion, probably the gas heater, shook this quiet, dead neighborhood.

     I called Teri. She picked up the phone, before the first burr had finished.

     "Teri?"

     There was a searching silence.

     "Caye?"

     I did not know what to say. I had never heard my name spoken in that way. She wasn't asking if it was me. She was asking if I was alive.

     "Caye?" she asked again. I did not know how to answer. And then she said one word. It came out quickly, filled with as much panic as with pity.

     "Go."

     Click.

XI.

With Nick and Ishi gone, I expected everything to come crashing down like a dynamited factory—a flash at the base, a loud crack, balloons of smoke, and the top collapses into rubble with wires sticking out.

But no, the disused, unused lot of my life was still standing.

Ishi, freighted with desire, and Nick, with the good will that sticks to the fortunate, for whom things just work out until they don't—they were the ones who believed in me, who sought me out to take them to her. Tricia Lifton survived, she outlasted fate, she had the secret. Without Ishi and Nick, fate was beckoning me into the end with a clerk's unfazed efficiency: just this way, just over there.

I walked under a pallid blue sky waiting for it to happen. In the parks, rusted tree tops were snarled with plastic carnage like deep sea creatures pulled up in a net. I went to libraries where trackers would never look for me, if any were still trying. I felt like a trespasser in a palace. I ran my fingers over the top of the books, feeling the solidity of pages pressed together, the coarse texture of one book's rough pages, the smooth filiations of another.

The first one I pulled out was light for something that looked like a squashed gray brick. The pages fanned open, imprinted with row upon row of black lines and curls. It had no illustrations, nothing to soothe the eye, the cover was gray and undecorated.

How can you spend so much time going over every letter, understanding every word, every sentence—where do you get the perseverance to read from beginning to end without getting bored by the same words coming up again and again?

Do you look away at something whole and curved like an opened umbrella just to relax your eye and give it a break from its back-and-forth track along the twenty, thirty, forty horizons? Or do you need something more lively—traffic, the movement of other people, a spaniel racing around a tree in pursuit of a squirrel—to relieve the monotony of twenty six letters repeated millions of times?

I sniffed it and was surprised by the smell, a background of morel and mold, the faint tint of a penny. How many fingers turned these pages? I put it back.

The next had a different character. Its pages were bright and white and full of photographs: men in hard hats scaled the scaffolding of a skyscraper; a police officer with white gloves directed traffic in a blur of cars; soldiers—Hussars, Cossacks— alive and lined up like toys in a child's fastidious arrangement. Maybe one of them had written the letters I found in the attic. I slid it back and walked on. My fingers tingled and felt dirty.

When the libraries closed, I sat on benches waiting for the end. The clouds rolled across the sky with nothing to say; it wasn't that they'd said anything before, but the shapeless shapes scrolling across the blue unstarred palimpsest took on a new silence, not the silence of a secret being kept, where the silence means that you are at least worth keeping a secret from, but the uncaring silence of death.

I stood on bridges, hoping that death would come up behind me and cosh me. A tumble into oblivion, off the edge of a horizon, my corpse carried out to sea or snagged in the reeds. Something was going to happen, I just didn't know what. I dreamt about it. I saw myself clutching my guts, dropping to my knees, rolling over, and flopping around like a fish, my face frozen in a scream, dirt sticking to my cheeks. And what would the people do? Would they think I was one of them having a fit? Would they run for help? Or would they know?

A dog barked, bounding after a stick flung by a boy. A car horn, a screech. The dog brought the stick back.

Or would they laugh? It would be funny. They wouldn't believe their luck, to see the last of us to go. They'd take snapshots as I flapped, stupidly dying, and publish them in the newspaper. Images unsuitable for their children, their lovely special children, little versions of them. Maybe I would detonate, my teeth and bone fragments spraying calcified shrapnel, blinding them, killing some, and making the rest feel disgusting and ashamed.

Sometimes I thought how I'd want it to be. Not gagging on my own death, like Ishi, or brutally, like Nick but along a seafront. In the hazy romance of dusk when things don't matter. I sit on a bench bleached the color of slate, marbled by gull droppings. Ishi, Nick, my father, my mother, the ghost of the letter writer walk past me. They glance adoringly and sadly at me, already missing me. Then they promenade down to a pier where gulls wheel overhead and they watch a flock of starlings, thousands swarming in the air, a fluttering cloud, darting like a school of black fish against the wash of the sun's last light. And I look into the distance, over and beyond the crashing waves, smile mysteriously, and just stop.

But nothing happened. I drank cold tea in styrene cups and walked in grim circuits. At night, I found cheap hostels and lay on the bed, staring at the ceiling, listening to the pulsing thump of a television, the muffled beat of people making love to themselves or each other.

On a rainy morning, I found a pen balancing across a sewage grate. Its reservoir was almost full and the tiny ball in its nib rolled smoothly under my thumb. I pocketed it for drawings.

Without Teri to give me ideas, I spent hours folding napkins and flattening them, waiting for inspiration, longing to hear Teri's voice tell me what to do, hoping that I would find something in myself without needing her. Other days, I would color in the whole napkin, running the nib as gently over the coarse tissue as a caterpillar's tread, back and forth until it was blue-black and looked like my father's painting; then I scraped away the ink-saturated strands to the white layer below and started again.

One afternoon I was in a café, finishing another napkin, so bored I almost wished it would happen: come take me, do it now, nobody would care, not even me.

"Hello?"

The voice seemed to be addressing me, but I didn't look up, I kept drawing.

"S'okay?"

I glanced up. "Is what okay?" I said, like I was looking for a fight. The man was grinning as if he expected me to recognize him. With a few jabs of his head, he indicated whether I minded him taking the seat across from me.

"Yes."

This delighted him. He sat, checking my blue napkin with a pout like he was judging a work of art, and, when he got the waitress's attention, ordered a tea and scone without saying a word, just by pointing. He got even more excited when the tea and scone were laid in front of him. A clap of his hands, thin fingers dancing against one another, and he tucked in. The scone was quickly gone, its crumbs squashed under his finger and transferred to his lips. Once in a while he glanced at me like he was still waiting for me to recognize him.

Finally he stood. I had not noticed how short he was, how boyish his body was, like someone had taken a middle-aged man's head, with thinning hair and gray stubble, and stuck it onto a teen's body.

"Meet me at the University."

I looked at him blankly. His friendliness softened, became less aggressive.

"Come down later, there's a lecture you might want to hear. I think it might mean something to you."

I shrugged.

"Good," he said, then he was gone. The woman behind the counter dragged his plate and empty cup of tea away. She came back.

"You gonna pay for him?"

I took a bus and got off at the university stop next to an old phone booth. The university was not what I expected. Lecturers and writers and people who became famous in geography, history, and philosophy taught here, investigating flora in the mountains and what it means to be an animal. We talked about places like this in our residences, listening to the older ones, all gone now, explain how people learned and drank, had sex, and made their way into the world. It was like hearing about a mystical world, an unfathomable place, spoken of with disgust and envy.

But I imagined something else, something I read in the letters; I had to be careful not to let any details slip, but I knew about a student dashing down ivy-padded lanes, interrupted on his way to sherry with professors by the chime of cathedral bells, such a pretty sound he had to stop to catch other students' eyes with the precious knowledge that they were young and free.

There was not a spire in sight. No trees, no hedges, no cloisters, no ivy, just rolling weather-resistant grass lawns cut up by broad gravel paths, a technically-designed space that implied a lawn but could never be used as such. No birds, no pigeons, no squirrels. No people. Across the commons lay a row of cinderblock buildings more like bunkers than cathedrals of learning. Heating fuel leaked from metal pipes, trailing black threads.

I knew it was a trap but I had hoped to see something from the letters, if anything was left of his world. The bus trundled away sending up a cloud of black smoke that fell across me. Still nothing. The air was cool, dissolving the exhaust fumes. We were far enough from the city for the air to be vaguely scentless. No gun oils, leather padding, sweating men in the winds.

The phone in the booth burred. At the fifth ring, I lifted the phone from the cradle.

"Come to the library," said a voice.

"Which building?"

"Wait a minute, you'll see me."

I hung up. Over by a glass-and-steel block, a man stepped out the front doors and waved.

I walked to him. He was short and stocky, the top of his head reaching my shoulders.

"I'm so pleased you've come," he said. "Does anybody know you're here?"

"Just the little guy," I said, then felt bad because they were the same height.

His eyes narrowed and he spoke under his breath. "Are there any others?"

I stared down at him.

"Never mind," he said and a smile came back. "You're with friends now. Come in."

He put his hand on my arm, pulled me through the weather-resistant doors, into a glass labyrinth of staircases and crooked levels, and led me to an auditorium in the lower level.

"Nobody will pay any attention to us," he whispered. "Oh, by the way, the name's Flinn."

Our seats were in the back row, held in reserve with a plump burgundy sweater. The cheerful scone-eater was in the adjacent seat. As soon as we arrived, he reclaimed his sweater without looking at us. The auditorium was packed. Every seat was taken and people lined the wall behind us. Most were students but there were a few who were older like Flinn and his friend. The room rattled with chatter.

I thought that it might happen here, in front of all these people, but I couldn't get up to leave because Flinn's arm was pressed against mine.

After a moment there was a tapping. The chief lecturer stood at the podium. A screen was illuminated behind him with the university's name and crest. He flicked the microphone like he was intrigued by it.

"There's no need for the screen," he mumbled, and peered down his nose at the control panel.

He pushed a button, the illumination faded, and the screen rose with nasty snaps and cracks, then stopped midway up the wall.

The lecturer looked at it sternly. There was nothing to do other than make faces at it.

As the hall quieted, he gave up on the controls, glanced up with mild surprise that the room was full of people, then welcomed us and introduced Leon Smiscka.

Smiscka sat at the side of the stage, smiling at the right times and cocking his head as his publications were listed. The lecturer finished with a stuttering invitation to the podium and bowed to Smiscka, who did not stand. Instead, he threw back his head, jutted his chin, and searched the ceiling. I looked up. A few other people did as well. Smiscka stared over our heads, his eyes darting here and there as if following an insect flitting in the high heavy air. The lecturer glided to his seat in the front row. As soon as he smoothed his gown and sat, Smiscka came together like a shattered glass vase reassembling itself in reverse.

"If you will forgive me," he said, "I will deliver my lecture from here, marginal to the stage but not to you. My back is killing me. Usually, when I stand at a podium for two hours, it is only a torture for my audience. Ha ha. But my back is killing me. That is how we put it, no? It is killing me. Perhaps I am killing it. We often get the two confused. What is killing us and what we are killing.

"My back is not killing me. It is punishing me. I picked up a child in play, forgetting that even little children can weigh fifteen kilos. They pack a lot of weight into their frames. A lifetime of guilt is compacted into a ball right here." He patted his belly. "They carry it around their whole lives, but it will get lighter as they digest it, releasing it with belches of lies and perjury.

"When I picked up the child, I bellowed in pain as my back gave way and the child thought it was part of the game. Children have no sympathy for the pain of adults. I collapsed, the child emulated me, proving once and for all that play is violence mitigated by ignorance of consequence, just as art is violence against meaning mitigated by ignorance of responsibility. The consequence for you, which the child remains ignorant of, is that I give my lecture from the chair here."

Everybody around me laughed. In the front row, they laughed hard.

"Can you hear me in the back?"

There was a satisfied murmur from those around me. Flinn nodded vigorously, if redundantly.

"Good. I have a responsibility even to those who belong in the rafters." They laughed again. Smiscka was cracking them up.

"Then I shall begin. Or perhaps I have already begun. I apologized, yes, when I asked your forgiveness. We are told an apology is a beautiful thing. It is a way of taking responsibility. But does it not retract itself? Is it not an admission of guilt that makes the guilt go away? A sort of perfection.

"I want to talk today about the perfectibility of the person, the striving that has been with us since the dawn of time, the promise that was uttered in the beginning with the logos, the word, the perfect word, which was only a promise of perfection. The perfect has become real, without the logos. This is the case that I will be making.

"Let us begin again, not with an apology but with a story that is all too familiar and yet which will soon become legend. We are witnesses to the end of a history and the beginning of a myth. The difference between the familiar historical and the legendary mythical is that we are always bored with the former and awaiting the latter.

"Here is how the myth will begin. In California, before the storms, professors come together with a biotechnology enterprise to license technologies that can engineer viruses to package and transmit human genes. In a display of audacity, they bring journalists and scientists into a room like this and take turns to stand at the podium to talk about what they are achieving. It is a unique partnership between the academe, private enterprise, and the military. They are not shy about this. They do not hide it. They announce it, they celebrate it, they advertise it with cartoons drawn by famous cartoonists.

"The viruses, they say, are like tourists with a suitcase they intend to leave in the country they visit, tourists who bring gifts, perhaps a suitcase filled with seeds, which will grow and flourish in the new land.

"And like tourists, the viruses are given a passport and a destination, a visa to the white blood cells and the marrow and the axons in our brains. And like tourists, they are only welcome for a brief period before they must leave.

"It is a happy vacation when we come home with the knowledge that we have made the world better. Is this not the fantasy that has driven history? You go as a tourist to enjoy the rest of the world and you are not a lout, you are not exploiting poverty and misery, you are bringing gifts as you get your much-needed break from a productive bourgeois life, and when you return you come back knowing that the natives are more enlightened because of your vacation. No?

"Two thousand families submit themselves to the first stage of research, only a few hundred are selected, and the results are fantastic. Sperm meets egg meets virus. Healthy children are born. By four years old, they are indistinguishable from their fellows, running around the playground, potty-trained, precocious. We have footage of these first ones; it has even appeared in pop videos, you know?

"When the children are five, the patents are sold to Grassley, who give an astronomical fee to the professors, to the scientists, and to the entrepreneurs. Nobody seems to notice that they pay the military nothing. Grassley goes into big business. They promise to put the genius in the genes. It is estimated that twenty thousand children are born with this technology.

"Jump forward and the first batch are excelling in everything they do. They are winning awards for their poetry and their sporting skills, they have handsome faces and are leaders, they are skilled writers, they are falling in love, they have gone on scholarships to universities around the world, and are distinguishable from their peers only by being so distinguished. And they begin to drop dead. Dozens a day. Over a period of days. They are going fast. What a mess.

"Everything stops. Grassley dissolves itself overnight, its executives say that they are not responsible, they were not scientists, they are not interested in a technology that causes harm. There are lawsuits and funerals and meetings. That was nearly twenty years ago. For nearly twenty years the Grassley children have approached adulthood, wave after wave, mown down at the barbed wire of late adolescence like soldiers leaving the trenches into enemy gunfire. The last batch, Grassley's last products, have approached their demise. And, let me risk the following: when they are extinct, human perfection dies with them.

"These are perfect beings, stronger, faster, better at everything. It is true they are despised. Tickers, counters. Who amongst you would take one home, let it sleep in your house? You would rather have foreigners in your home than these hated creatures. Who amongst you voted against a politician because he voted for the Cloning Segregation Act?"

Two or three hands went up. The Chief Lecturer did not raise his hand.

"I know, I know, most of you are too young. It is your parents' fault. You would have protested the act and it is true that some did."

On either side of me, Flinn and his friend nodded vigorously.

"Some did not want to relegate these perfect beings to isolation. And yet it is true that we bred a perfect generation— which we made a generation of slaves. They were not our slaves, though it is possible that is how they were intended. We have no word from the military on that account. Why did the military not receive a penny from Grassley? How many of them were created by the enterprise between Grassley and the military? How many, if any, were the so-called 'killers'?

"Maybe they were military slaves, maybe not, but we know for sure they were slaves to our desire for perfection. Let me risk my first interpretation: creating perfection was an apology for our history of imperfection. We made them just as God made Adam and Eve, but not to populate the world in His likeness. No, because we could not make amends for our fall the old-fashioned way, we did so with our fallen ingenuity.

"Ha, do not worry. You can account for this myth using any other language, not just the language of God. We produced them in the world as more-evolved beings by harnessing not the mechanics of evolution but by technologizing the potential in evolution itself. We made them to make amends for how we—in God, in nature—are not good enough.

"Now let us be honest. We despise apologies. We despise it when we must face our guilt even when we retract it. They were our apologies for our imperfection and so we despised them, more than we despise our children. Some of you laugh. Maybe it is because what you recognize what I say is true, maybe because you think it absurd. Isn't it funny that we cannot tell the difference. Yes, we despised them more than our own children, they were proxies for the hatred we bear for children, which is always hidden. What lucky people we were! The first to have real proxies for the most unspeakable, ubiquitous hatred we have for children. We let them know, oh, how we tortured them! The ones who were bred for cognitive skills, we gave them old computers and made them count. They spent their lives counting meaninglessly in front of computers. They did not know it. That too is a type of perfection: reducing productivity to its essential pointlessness, not the least of which was their ignorance of the pointlessness. And we had a joke. We called them counters. We defined them by their pointlessness."

I became dizzy. Ishi was doing nothing? She was pointless?

"It is true that we ensured that after the first generation, they were not instructed in how to read. They were not invited to the written word, forbidden the book as it is written. You know the reason well, it is our little secret."

I was spinning, trying to hold onto the words, which were flinging me away a like a child unloosed from a carousel.

"The secret is famous. But what is the real secret? The secret within the secret? We prevented them from reading to keep a secret, as if they were exalted and must be protected from the truth, like little innocents, like pure children, and yet the secret within this secret is: Was this not guaranteed to make them lesser than us, and, in exiling them from the written word, make them lesser in this world? A man whose name I will not mention, you know who I talk about, but I refuse to cite him even as I quote him, he calls them 'illiterate worms'.

"These worms, these least amongst us, were the perfect humans because they were slaves to the desire for perfection, perfectly so. It began with the logos, a promise. Our contract with perfectibility, our promise of perfectibility, was written in them. And they cannot read. And because they cannot read, they were not perfect, the contract is unwritten, and so we were unable to read the contract with perfection that we wrote, the promise was broken as it was spoken. The exemption from the logos is returned to the logos, the apology is no longer a retraction of guilt but a confession without any hope of forgiveness. No wonder we hate them. It is not they who are illiterate in their illiteracy, but us because we cannot read what we wrote in them. They are not an apology for our imperfection, but an apology revoked: they are a reproach."

At this point, I could take no more. I tried to get up. Flinn sensed the movement. His hand clamped down on my thigh.

"What is left? There is a twist. Their perfection endures not despite but because of the error we made in making them imperfect, not our intentional mistake in making them illiterate but our unintentional mistake in making them brutally and certainly mortal. They have a relationship with death as that which inevitably comes before adulthood that puts them into a world beyond the one we can ever know, even as the very last ones live, breathe, touch, feel, smell, see, and taste. All that enters us enters them. Rays of light, chocolate—you know I have a fondness for chocolate—water, and the like. And yet everything that enters them dies on the altar of their martyrdom, not just food and chocolate, but sin and hatred and spite. It is not that they lack senses, no; it is not that they lack literacy, no; it is that they lack the essential unknown that makes us who we are; they lack the inability to read fate's script that compels us to comprehend the mysteries; they lack the essential ambiguity in the logos that underwrites all legibility, that creation bears within it an unknown destruction. It is true, if a ticker could read, he or she could still not read.

"But let me risk my final interpretation: what they lack is, in a word, a soul. A soul: the imperfection within us, for which we always apologize. A soul: the spirit of imperfection which is why it alone transcends the perfection of death. A soul: which is why we are the masters, they the slaves. And then we reach a conclusion. Without a soul, without its moral imperfection, they are moral perfection."

Smiscka's words ceased to have meaning; they were merely measured sounds, rasping lyrics in a foreign language. I suddenly felt tired and closed my eyes. A memory came back. A recent one. After I shot my father I walked to the car as the flames spread through my father's house. Nick was in the driver's seat, sound asleep, his chin on his chest, arms folded. I opened the door. He was not buckled in. One of his arms fell to his side and he jerked awake. I grabbed his arm and yanked him out. He tumbled out onto the lawn, confused and hurt. I knelt beside him, held his neck down and pushed the gun against the back of his skull. One shot ended Nick. I wiped my hands, wiped Nick from my shirtsleeve and left the gun beside him.

It was an act of kindness.

When the lecture was over there was time for questions. Students lined up at a microphone. Flinn nodded and we slipped out the back of the auditorium. The scone-eater followed. Outside, he introduced himself as Eric. I was right about them, although I did not know what I knew—only that I was right.

A few minutes later we were in a cramped room in a house behind the university. Flinn lit candles and put on creepy music and Eric sat on a bed, rolling a spliff. The room was crowded with books, bottles, and a sheet hung over the window. They were like students but they were too old. Eric offered me the spliff but I declined.

Flinn spoke, meditating on history in the flickering, smoky light. He said they were in the department of political philosophy and members of an organization that fought for the rights of tickers. I didn't react but that might have been confirmation enough.

He said they were not interested in Smiscka's philosophy, he said we were innocents who had suffered from the drive for profit, babes produced by the union of warmongers and imperialists. He waited for me to say something so I shrugged, although there was one question I had.

He said it was risky, what they were doing. Stiff penalties, prison time, shame for their families, this had happened to people. And all the time, Eric smoked and made gestures to show he agreed or to remind Flinn of this or that.

It was all so forced. And then I wanted to ask them if they knew where Tricia Lifton was. And as soon as I was about to ask, I knew it was all over. I opened my mouth to speak.

"Here, listen to this." It was Flinn, by the radio. He puzzled over the dial as classical music played.

Eric again offered me the spliff, grinning like a moron. This time I took it, regarded it.

"Who do trackers work for?" I asked. "Grassley or the government?"

The grin dropped off Eric's face and he fell backwards on the bed, fumbling under the pillow.

Before he could find what he was looking for, I was beside him. I shoved the spliff into his eye, grinding the hot grain into his eyeball with my thumb. He clutched his face and screamed. An ashen blister formed on the belly of my thumb.

I turned to Flinn who was coming at me with a knife. A feint to the left, a step to the right, and the knife was past me. My knee cracked his ribs above his liver. I could feel one of the bones snap, a dagger gouging his organs.

Eric was flopping on the bed like a fish, holding his face. I took the gun from his fingertips, cocked it, and ended Eric with a loud pop.

"Who do you work for?"

Flinn was whimpering on the floor, his feet pedaling in agony.

"Are you trackers?"

The music came to an end. I had no more time. I shot him in the head, knocked over the candles, made sure the sheet over the window caught fire, and let myself out.

XII.

It was raining every day. I phoned Teri but hung up when she answered. I used public phones and stood in the booths, my hand attached to the phone after I ended the call. Fat drops rolled down the glass. I looked absently at the streets, glossy in the showers, and waited. No police cars swerved in to surround me. I found myself waiting longer. Waiting to be caught. Waiting for the grip of plastic cuffs. A hand jamming my shirt collar into my ear. A shove face-first into the littered back seat of a car. Nothing. I was no closer to anything but the end.

Two days later, I was recognized. But not by trackers.

Armond burst in front of me like he came out of thin air. I almost didn't recognize him.

"Caye?" He cried happily. "We found you." And then more solemnly: "Heard about Ishi." And, just as solemnly, "Have you heard about the others?"

I shook my head. He held my arms and looked at me. I felt like crying. The passersby paid us no attention. They were just getting on with their shopping, coming back from work or picking up kids or whatever. Armond steered me into a café, to a table where you could stand to look over the street. There was a newspaper opened in front of him. It was upside down. I turned it around to avoid suspicion.

"You're lucky," said Armond, excitedly. "You remember Kara and Jacob?"

Before I had time to answer, Kara appeared. I remembered her. I could tell that her surprise was not only at seeing someone new but the surprise of seeing me. She looked the same as I remembered: greasy brown hair around her fine-boned face like a fragile, beautiful tramp.

"Caye," she said in a low, sing-songy voice, "Sorry about Ishi."

I knew she wasn't being sarcastic but she always sounded that way.

"And here's Jacob," said Armond, getting even more excited and bouncy.

I remembered him too. Pushing through the crowd with an enormous green duffel bag that had him almost doubled over, he was even bigger than me, too intense for his own good, driven by something that had him carrying twice his weight on his back. He busted into the cafe, immediately making it feel smaller. Ignoring us, he dropped his duffel to the floor.

After giving me a once up-and-down, he said, "Sorry about Ishi."

"Why don't you come along," said Armond to me. "We've got something you might be interested in."

In a nearby parking lot, Armond made a shooting move with the electronic key at his hip like a gunfighter in a duel. A chipper red vehicle awoke and flashed its yellow eyes.

In the backseat next to Kara, I crumpled and words emptied from my skull. The universe was a book of scrambled letters and spaces and some of them fell together in a way that made sounds—cracking, thunder, snaps—but if words were formed it was only by accident. The weight of exhaustion crashed over me. It was all I could do to keep my eyes open. Closing them felt like coming home. Nothing else. Nothing at all.

A finger stroked my shoulder. "We're almost there."

"Where?"

Kara wrinkled her nose and whispered in my ear. "There."

My eyelids felt cast in lead.

Jacob hulked over the steering wheel. Armond's energy had left him and he sank in the seat.

Kara stared out the window with the affectionate contempt of someone who could look down on nature itself. She smelled like sour milk. The car spun along the side roads. My head nodded approval to every rut and pothole. The stiffness in my neck attested to that.

The sun came up over the stubble of farmland. We turned onto a dirt road over a cattle grille and bounced along the track, past a copse of elders, pulling up to a farmhouse decked out with rustic touches: a wheelbarrow on the lawn, hoes and shovels standing to attention along the wall of a barn. The windows were dark, the walls clutched by a rose bush. A shaggy dog loped across the grass, its barks punching holes into the air.

A woman met us and let us in a side door, a relic made of white painted stiles, black metal hinges, and a latch that you lifted. The dog pushed past us to get inside first.

The house was quiet and old and you could smell the farm in it. The hay, the manure. Armond kicked off his boots and charged into a room where he dove onto a sofa and began snoring, first as a joke and then for real. Jacob took a seat and filled it, his head back. The woman pointed to a narrow flight of stairs.

At the top was a single room. There was one bed with a yellow-and-white quilt. Daylight was coming through the window. Kara drew the curtain across the bar. The room became darker, not dark, but dark enough to sleep in. She closed the door.

"I love sleeping in the day when I'm as tired as this," she said.

She helped me out of my jacket.

"Have you been alone?" she asked, then went on without waiting for me to answer. "I went to the mountains with Armond. And Parker and Sofia. Do you remember them?" She pulled my shirt up around my chest, but wasn't tall enough to pull it over my head. "They gave up. I think that's how we end, we just give up, don't you think?"

She seemed old. So did Armond and Jacob. She lay me down and ran her fingers through my hair. I fell through a thick black cloud into the vaporous nothing beneath it, nothing at all, not a whisper, not a dream, not a glimmer of memory, nothing but warmth and the rustle of fingers stroking my hair.

After a day and a night of sleep and a bath, we were puffy-faced and hungry. The woman brought in a pitcher of milk from the cows. Jacob cracked a dozen eggs into a bowl, ground in pepper and salt, and started beating them.

Armond took out an envelope.

Kara gave him a hard stare, clamped her hand over

Armond's, and looked suspiciously at me.

"Caye's got to know," he said.

Kara glanced at Jacob but he was pretending to pay no attention. He addressed himself to buttering the toast with a ferocity of distraction and hunger.

"We've got something," said Armond.

Kara got up, flighty and panicked, and fled the room. Jacob thrashed the eggs. His huge frame was shaking.

"What?" I asked, dreading the answer.

"Her!" Armond held out his hands like he was welcoming me to a party. Disappointed that I didn't react, he continued, "Long story or short? Okay, short. We know where she is. We met a guy who told us about a place by the water where they're keeping somebody, he said we'd know who he meant. She's there." He sat back, raised an eyebrow. Jacob poured the eggs into a pan. Armond waited for the sizzle to quiet.

"The thing is, Caye, we're—" He couldn't say it. "They plan to keep her away from us, just 'til we're—you know. When we're gone, they let her go."

Kara returned, tight-lipped, composing herself. Jacob slid a plate in front of each of us. The omelet was perfectly yellow, daubed orange with melted strands of cheddar. The room smelled like hot drawn butter, sweet egg, hayseed breeze, and the toothpaste Kara used. She sipped coffee, and I couldn't smell the toothpaste anymore.

Jacob ate a mouthful of omelet. Armond pretended to give up on impressing me and attacked the egg with a fork. Kara tried not to cry.

I pushed away the omelet. "Why don't you say it."

Armond kept eating like he hadn't heard me. Jacob poked at his egg and spoke to the others, though he was speaking to me.

"They can make tickers that don't disappear. But if we get there first—"

I tossed my fork onto the plate. It clattered and Kara jumped.

"You idiots are talking about Tricia Lifton, aren't you?" They froze when I said her name. "You can't even say her name but you're going to find her? You really believe they've got her? Because some man told you?"

"I can see why you don't believe," said Armond, "What about this?"

He finished his egg, wiped his mouth on his sleeve, and opened the envelope. He removed two small photographs and slid them across the table.

"What do you see?"

I picked up the photographs. It was her. The eyes, the cheeks, the bouffant hair. I had never seen either photo before.

"Where did you get these?" I asked and pushed them back.

"Like I said, we met a man." And then he stopped.

The mood changed. Jacob finished his eggs and scraped toast across the plate but he was on edge. Kara picked at the food, took small bites from her fork, and looked away.

I realized what was going on. They'd been acting like they had something I wanted, something they were keeping from me. But it was the other way around. They wanted me. They dangled her in front of me and I didn't bite. I pulled the plate towards me and began eating the eggs.

Finally Armond spoke. "Maybe you can help," he said. "You have nothing to lose, right?"

I finished my eggs before I responded. "Help you do what?"

"For starters, do you know where we can get weapons?"

I thought about it for a moment.

"Yes."

It took us the better part of a week to arrive at La Verde and it wasn't until the worst part of nightfall that we reached the station. The storm blasted by, swatting the car like an impatient giant shaking it to see if anything desirable was inside. It was pitch black with flashes on the horizon, far beyond where Ishi and I camped.

At the station, Jacob took a crooked iron from his duffel. I led the way and pushed through the door. The room was lit by whatever machines were working: the red flicker of the radar, the faded glow of computer screens in sleep mode, the haze that comes off electronic equipment. The two grizzled deputies were asleep at their terminals, as motionless as if they had their throats cut by nocturnal desert spirits.

Jacob stood between them and unleashed a swing of his pipe. The crack of iron against skull sent the first deputy to the floor. The other shuddered awake. Jacob brought the pipe down on his bald crown. Another crack, a shuffle to the floor, another dead deputy.

We removed the rifles and pistols, scopes, laser sights, ammunition.

There was no point cleaning or burying them or remembering that these men were fathers, husbands, beloved friends, and all the other things that can't be thought about at times like that.

We waited. Armond and Kara slept in one cot, Jacob took the other. I was not tired. When I was sure they were asleep, I searched the bench for my initials. At first, I thought they were lost, as if my signature, my twinned letters, had loosened, unshaped and unlettered into a pair of grooved worms that wriggled into the scrawled garden. Untended, unread, the letters twisted apart and returned to privacy, unspooling, quivering then recomposing themselves as scribble.

But no, the thumbnail-gouged *CM* was still there, just not where I remembered; the letters had stepped to the right. They were softer now, my butt-smoothed initials.

At dawn, I was stroking them when a jeep crunched over the gravel. The others woke instantly. They leveled their rifles behind the table. I stayed on the bench.

Noah and Meyers walked in, arguing. They saw the jiggling red beams of the laser sights and died surprised.

Meyers spun when I shot him from the bench. Noah fell against the door with bloody pockmarks in his forehead and leaned on the jamb like he had passed out happy, fat and drunk. The back of his skull splattered black and wet alongside Meyer's corpse like a glistening shadow.

What are you doing?" Armond asked.

I was going through Noah's jacket.

"Thought so."

I pulled a paper bag from his pocket.

"Breakfast."

We ate their doughnuts. Jacob went outside and turned off the jeep.

Kara turned to me. I knew what she was going to ask.

"One more," I said. "The chief'll be here soon."

The shot was expected and a surprise. It screeched in and hit its mark. Kara looked out the sliver of a window through her scope.

"There," she whispered.

She aimed and fired. The blast ebbed and the background fizz of the desert became audible again, a silence of sorts.

"Got him," she murmured.

We had tied Meyers to a chair with a rifle in his hand, baring his forehead. His scalp had a nasty purple and yellow gash but we cocked a hat over it. The chief took the bait. Did a good job too. Meyer's forehead was blasted open, his skull gray and spiky at the back like broken pottery.

Kara hopped down. She inspected Meyer's head, pausing to admire the chief's accuracy.

The morning air was fresh compared to the sticky sweetness of the station and its already-rotting corpses. The chief lay alongside scrubby plants, one of his legs in a black pool of sand that might have been darkened from the storm or his blood. He inched back and forth, his fingers playing an invisible piano above his head.

"Where'd the shot go?"

We searched for it. Kara pouted and kicked at the stubbly grasses. She knew what she was doing.

"Oh," Armond muttered. He reached down in the folds of the chief's crotch and pulled the fabric taut. There it was. A perfect shot to the upper inner thigh, straight through the femoral artery. You can't fight after a shot like that. Unbelievable pain. Your blood draining frantic pulses every second, filling up the planes of meat in the pelvis and thigh. The piano playing slowed.

"Good shot," Jacob said. Now that she was being admired, Kara came back to earth and gave me a shy look.

The chief looked up at me, his mouth and tongue working.

"Yes, it's me," I said.

His lips were white and his eyes met mine.

"You didn't think we'd meet again," I said. "You didn't think I was going to be the one watching you die."

He opened his mouth and rasped, "The world's full of surprises."

How could I not smile?

Death flapped down, a broken-winged bird tumbling to earth and came to a rest on the chief. No more silent piano music.

We set about ransacking the station. I opened a file cabinet. At the bottom, a coffee mug stood on a stack of folders. I tossed the coffee cup against the wall. It didn't break but a cake of dried coffee fell out. I scattered the papers on the floor. Something caught my eye. I kicked away the papers and picked up a photograph. It was of two bodies. The pair who had been lost. They were lying naked in the sand, twisted and shot up. Clipped to the photo was a card that identified them by name. It said they were murdered by bandits. Case closed. So that's what happened. I always hoped that they had escaped.

Armond and Kara kicked things over, stamped over the footprints in the dust outside, which didn't matter because the next rain would wash them away. After a fair warning, Jacob fired the deputies' pistols into the walls, the computers, the broken monitors. The station was smashed and bloody like it was attacked by fugitives.

An hour later we were on the road. We threw their wallets and watches and rings out the window. Our destination was fifteen hours away, so we aimed to find somewhere to sleep.

That evening, I did a drawing. It was predictable, as if Teri was standing over my shoulder and asked me to do it: a raven perched on the chief's shoulder. But it hadn't come from Teri. It came from me. The first thing I drew of my own accord.

Kara didn't like it. She frowned and rubbed her ear against her shoulder. A grinning, wide-jawed man, handsome and tough, was not how she planned to remember him. She didn't plan on remembering him at all. I got his nose right, his jaw, his eyes, but not his mouth. Every way I drew a line for a lip, it was wrong, like he was talking and I kept missing where the lip should be.

Kara slipped into the bathroom to take a shower. I stared at the picture. It didn't matter; and with that thought, joy filled me. I trembled and breathed faster. It's happening, I thought, it's finally happening—but I knew it wasn't. It was something else.

"I am Caye Mallory," I said aloud, just to slow my breathing. I couldn't bear the sound of my name and repeated it silently until it became fact, something other than me.

Kara returned in a t-shirt. When she saw me, she stopped in her tracks like she saw a ghost. She looked pretty and scared and dropped the towel on the floor and stumbled towards me. As she came close, she plucked the picture from my hand, tripped across the room, and placed it face down on the bedside table.

The chief and his raven were buried there.

She came back more steadily, stood behind me, and slid an arm around my shoulders, throwing the other around my neck so that it dangled in front of me. Our cheeks were touching and in the mirror it was like we were watching strangers watch us back. She turned first. Her nose traced circles on my cheek. Her breath was sweet like tomatoes. I watched a dry lip brush coarsely across the corner of my mouth.

I turned away from our reflection. Open mouths, round and fleshy with a hot hollow, an encounter without any shyness, just curiosity and loss.

I stood and we kissed each other's face, neck, ears, and her warmth lined up against me. She reached for the light.

Stroking my cheek in the dark, she asked, "Are you thinking of Ishi?"

It was only a remnant of humanity within me that prevented me from blurting out, "Who?"

A while later—no, it wasn't a while later. It was before we were done. Kara was above me. I was staring up at the fibrously-pimpled ceiling, listening to her take short breaths. There was scratching at the door. She didn't hear. I ran the back of my fingers over her nipples. She breathed faster, her body rocking against me. I closed my eyes. The door creaked open, she moaned. It closed. I began to burn, my thighs trembled. Kara collapsed on top me, her hair in my face. The burning became intense. She clutched my shoulders.

While she was in the bathroom, I pulled on my underwear and trousers and a sweater. The letters in the attic never spoke of this. They mentioned a friend's sister, blushes, courtship, the bittersweet misery of being apart, the joy of reunions, but that was it.

I walked into the cool night. There were no stars, the highway lights were out, and the motel sign was broken, only "-cy" was lit in purple.

Leaning against the wall was Armond. He was purple from the neon sign. I leaned against the wall beside him. A few doors down, someone was listening to music and singing along. There were four other cars and a truck parked along the low wall skirting the lot.

"Why'd you turn the paper round?" he asked, jamming his hands in his pockets.

"What paper?" I thought he meant my drawing.

"In the café. The newspaper. You turned it around."

He didn't say anything for a while. As my eyes adjusted to the night, he faded into the wall, out of the purple neon. I could smell the petroleum fumes from the cars settling into their sleep, and the greenish smells of coolant, and Armond's breath, his body.

"You can read," he said. We were quiet. "Is that your secret?" he leaned forward, his face purple again.

I said nothing.

"If they knew, they'd think you're a tracker." He waited for me to protest. "Jacob always thought you were a doll. A big doll. But Kara and I don't think so. You know?"

"No. I don't know."

"We thought—"

"What?"

"I can't say it."

"That I'm a killer?"

"Better get sleep," he said, relieved that I said it. "Tomorrow's the big day."

I nodded and he was gone, a glowing purple idiot switched off in the shadows. When I got into bed, Kara shifted over next to me, and we kissed before falling asleep.

XIII.

We made our way over sandy hillocks by foot, crossed trenches of foam-coated seawater, and passed an abandoned sewage plant, its spew long dissolved into the ocean.

When we were within a quarter mile of the depot, we slithered to the top of a dune and scattered sand over our back. From a distance, the depot was isolated and charmless, a depressed, dangerous place, a windowless breezeblock stadium planted in the wafting reeds and dunes like a giant shark suspended in the water, no motion, all menace. An old radar tower was dark, its antennae unmoving like weathervanes on a windless day. A rusty long-haul truck had backed up against an offloading bay. A man moved from the rear compartment into the building and back.

Gulls circled, starving, searching for scraps. One of them spotted us and swooped, hoping we were drowned porpoises, something dead and sea-softened, with eyes ripe for plucking.

Armond pulled a rubber band from a breast pocket, found a pebble, and fired it. The gull flew away, making sounds like it was laughing.

"What is the plan?" I whispered.

"Plans are bound to fail," said Armond.

I didn't understand, but Kara looked at me like I was stupid. "You never asked for the plan."

"I thought you didn't trust me, I thought that's why you didn't tell me the plan." My voice broke into something louder than a whisper. "Are you saying that the reason you didn't tell me the plan is because there isn't one?"

Armond chewed on his lip for a second and then frowned. "But you never asked," he said.

I broke into laughter. The people were idiots but we were worse.

We waited for another hour, watching the man go in and out of his truck empty-handed. There were no other souls. The gulls with black boomerang wings circled, the hazy sky darkened and pins of cold rain pricked out faces. Kara's fingers eventually found mine.

"It's now or never, right?" said Armond.

"Why not?" said Kara, releasing my hand.

One by one we climbed over the crest and slid through the brambles on our backs, holding rifles across our chests. Getting in was easy. Jacob crept up behind the man as he got into his lorry and broke his neck.

Then things did not go so well.

Kara limped into the room. She clutched her side, dark and shiny. Drying blood decorated her hands and forearms with red and black runes. Jacob followed, holding Armond, who was not dead, not yet. His arm dragged limp, dripping blood, and he had spit and blood on his face. His feet dragged over the tiles, pointing in the same direction. Jacob held Armond's arm around his neck as if they were supporting each other. He stumbled, then righted himself, which made Armond wince. They looked at me, rifles askew, bloodied, and waited for instructions.

"We're close," I said. I was unhurt.

And then for a moment we were ourselves again. We stood still, breathing heavily, looking at one another. The silence was familiar, our way of saying goodbye. Kara was the first to turn. She put her hand on the wall and let out a low growl of frustration and pain, shivering with fury.

Armond looked as though he wanted to say something, but he may have been choking. Jacob had been shot in the gut and was bleeding down his trousers. He shook his head at me. He didn't want Armond to know. I looked at Armond. He looked dead. I looked back at Jacob. He didn't know this yet.

I think it might have been funny. To get this close.

"Let's go," I said. Kara steadied herself, then pushed out the door. Jacob and Armond hobbled behind and I followed.

The doors were numbered. 201, 203, 205. We stopped.

207. Contamination Suite.

We could hear muffled alarms, bracketed by distance, but in the hall, there was only our breathing, fast, excited. I knelt beside the door, placed my empty rifle on the floor, removed a pair of pistols and held them out in front of me.

Jacob lay Armond against the wall. Kara leaned against the door listening. She nodded.

Jacob kicked the door open.

The first shot blasted the door shut. The second blew the bottom of the door off, ripping it from the hinge. Jacob bore the brunt in his knees and thighs, but Armond's body was hit too. Kara tried to kick the broken door open again, but the third blast followed too quickly—there was more than one person inside—and Kara flew at me like a cat attacking with claws and bared fangs. She grasped me, then fell away and her body rolled heavily on the floor. She lay in a fine mist of plaster and smoke.

There was no fourth blast, just the high snaps of pistol fire.

I watched, damp from Kara's spray.

Armond, who always had more energy than anybody else, was not dead yet. He lay across the broken doorway, pistols bucking in his hands. Most of the shots were going into the room but he was also hitting the door, the wall, the floor. Then he shuddered and spurted red and stopped.

Jacob sat across from the door, looking at the mangled mess of his waist and legs. Off to his side, holes appeared in the wall, *pop pop*, patiently working their way towards him, *pop pop*.

"I knew it'd be you, Caye," he said. He inspected the holes as they approached. One popped into his right shoulder, the next into his chest. He looked surprised and coughed. The next hit him in the forehead and that was it.

I looked at Armond, drained and dead, at Jacob, huge and dead, and at Kara, emptied and dead. Steam came from their plaster-dusted bodies.

I walked into the room. It was ruined with overturned tables and chairs and plaster blown from the walls. A bitter fog hung and twisted in the air.

A tracker jumped up and I shot him. Another fired, clipping my arm, and I shot him twice. A third pointed his gun from behind a table and I shot him through the wood, first in the leg then in the neck.

A pair of deputies lay wounded and moaning, and I fired two times, and all of them were dead.

In the only remaining chair sat a figure. It was a human form in a bulletproof vest—a dummy.

They put a wig on it.

It's like they knew we were idiots.

XIV.

The air was getting cold and the streets emptied. They
said a dozen people died a year from cold snaps. A few were
suicides but most were people who were locked out.

The library was open early. A security guard stood in
front of the glass sliding doors. He wore a blue-knit sweater with
a badge and a herald sewn too low. He paid me no mind as I
circled the brick pavilion once, twice, with my collar up. I came
around a third time and he was in the same place.

He leaned against a column, crushing a cigarette under
his heel, then removed a plastic thimble of cream from his
pocket and poured it into his coffee. He had zipped up his
overcoats. I could smell the sour tang of tobacco on his fingers.
He coughed dry smoke and sucked the top layer of his coffee. I
wondered why he was waiting. The freeze was coming.

"Hey," he said after I passed. I didn't turn. I kept going
towards the doors.

"Hey," he said louder. I turned. A newspaper vendor was
handing him a folded newspaper. The guard gave the vendor
some coins. Trapped between the coins was a plastic filament
stripped from a pack of cigarettes. The temperature was falling.
The vendor calculated distances to the office block across the
road. The guard reached to pick the filament from the coins in
the vendor's flat, dirty palm. He rolled it into a loose ball and
flicked it onto the ground. The vendor pocketed the change and
jogged across the street, clutching his papers, his breath
steaming. We watched him enter the building.

I turned back to the entrance. The electric doors didn't
open. I waved at my reflection to resuscitate the dead sensor,
then pried the glass doors apart. I entered and let them clunk
back. I heard a whoosh behind me. The doors wouldn't open for
me but they opened for the ghost following me. A gust of chilled
wind entered. The doors closed.

The guard was still outside, watching me. He had pulled
on his hat and his goggles. There was no more steam from his
coffee. He checked the newspaper then looked at me, back and

forth. He dropped the newspaper and stepped up against the doors, still holding the coffee in one hand, and with the other rummaging through his pockets. The doors opened for him. He entered with a burst of ice air. I removed the pen I had been using for my drawings and jammed it into his neck. He fell backwards, the doors closed, then sealed as the temperature plummeted. His blood froze around him. The coffee rolled out of the cup. There was a click and the interior doors opened.

The library was high-ceilinged with tall thin windows secured by vertical iron bars that curled back on themselves. The bookshelves rose to just above my head. The weight of literature, the density of trapped language, settled the books along the bottom of a vast room filled with the liquidy silence when all the words are collected into tiny black marks and clamped shut.

In the center was a semi-circular circulation desk. Two quiet old men sat behind the booth. One of them read a newspaper, the other leaned over a book, turning a page every few seconds. He lifted it for a better look. It was by Smiscka. He reached for his mug and raised his eyes to glance over the book at me. I decided not to smile. He smiled anyway. As his eyes flicked back to his book, I went to the computer terminals and sat.

Teri said to meet in the library. It wasn't for the books. She told me to use the computers. I would find what I needed to know then she would meet me in the children's section. There was a harsh wooden scrape, a chair pulled along the floor.

The computer demanded a password.

"Literature," said a man's voice. It was one of the old men from the circulation desk. "The password is 'literature'," he said. He laughed soundlessly like it was a joke I should get, and I typed it in: L-I-T-E-R-A-T-U-R-E.

The computer was pleased. It blinked and revoked its blue screen. Up fluttered a backdrop: a photograph of a cottage with a trellis and a garden; it was where I would grow old, where I would receive letters from a nephew who sent long hand-written letters because he knew I read every word he wrote as he made friends and had adventures and fell in love, and I would never expect the letters to come to an abrupt end, because such things never happen.

At the top corner were the options. I picked one and the cottage was swallowed by a dark screen with white lozenges offering search options.

The two old men behind the circulation desk were whispering. I could hear the rustling of a newspaper, snatched from hand to hand and held still. They were debating whether the picture was me. They couldn't believe it, they didn't believe it, they were wondering what to do.

I typed her name and hit return. The muscles in my hands and forearms twitched as if I had been digging through the soil to get here, my neck was tight from the burrowing. I wanted the two men to see me when I found her. A set of digits appeared in the center of the screen, counting rapidly.

50%. 77%. 100%.

Newspaper columns slid upwards across the screen with golden block six letters long. I did not read whether 'Tricia' or 'Lifton' was highlighted, I just waited—there. A golden box was twice the length. Both words highlighted. Her whole name.

I found her. I found Tricia Lifton.

Barely breathing, I held the edge of the table to steady myself as I, I alone amongst us, I, the last one, I, Caye Mallory, the only one who could read, read:

Dear Sir:

If they knew what lies in store for them, the clones would surely kill themselves en masse. All societies contain prohibitions against suicide even in such dire circumstances and our society would be ill-served biologically, evolutionarily, or morally by rampant suicide. They must live to meet their fate just as we all must. To accomplish this, we must find a way of giving them hope, enough hope to endure what lies ahead.

Yours sincerely,
Tricia Lifton

Books by Saul Wheelock

Human Sushi

Tricia Lifton

10.32, 10.33, 10.34

An Ethnography of the Spirit World

Questions, comments, compliments, critiques:

saulspinners@gmail.com

www.ingramcontent.com/pod-product-compliance
Lightning Source LLC
Chambersburg PA
CBHW071343130626
46556CB00005B/2007